D1457619

BOOK TWO

USA TODAY BESTSELLING AUTHOR

BROOKE O'BRIEN

TYSIN

USA Today Bestselling author Brooke O'Brien takes you out on tour with A Rebels Havoc in this brother's best friend, close proximity rock star romance.

Tysin Briggs is a player.

He's cocky, selfish, and sexy as sin. I've heard the rumors, and it's no secret, he's just as talented in the bedroom as he is on the guitar.

As the lead guitarist for A Rebels Havoc, and my brother's best friend, Tysin has heartbreak written all over him. We were asking for trouble sneaking around behind my brother's back. It still didn't stop me from spending the summer with him or from falling in love with him.

Two years have passed since he destroyed my heart, crushing it into a million pieces. A lot has changed since then, including the ring on my finger. When my brother asks for my help filling in as the manager of their sold-out tour, it's an opportunity I can't refuse.

I should've known the past wouldn't stay in the past.

But what I didn't count on was how hard it would be to resist him.

Thank you for reading **TYSIN**! I hope you love Tysin and Kyla's story as much as I do.

You can join my Facebook group, Brooke O'Brien's Rebel Readers Group, to discuss the series and get sneak peeks on future releases. Sign up for my newsletter to find out more about my new releases. To join, visit: www.authorbrookeobrien.com/followbrooke

Happy reading!

AUTHOR'S NOTE

Dear Reader,

Thank you for grabbing your copy of Tysin.

Like real life, Tysin and Kyla are far from perfect. They make morally gray decisions and their story deals with subjects that may be sensitive for some readers. If you're looking for a safe romance, this book is not for you.

If you prefer to start at the beginning of Tysin and Kyla's story, be sure to check out Sins of a Rebel. This book is an *optional* prequel novella and does end in a cliffhanger.

While the rest of the A Rebels Havoc series can be read as stand-alones, if you prefer to read in order, it's recommended you start with Brix as the stories to interconnect.

You can find all my books, along with the recommended reading order, on my website at: www.authorbrookeobrien.com.

I hope you love Tysin and Kyla as much as I do! Happy reading!

Brooke

DEDICATION

To my beta readers, who held on through the rollercoaster of writing this story. Thank you for always supporting me endlessly. And to me, for not giving up on Tysin and Kyla, even when they tried to give up themselves.

CHAPTER ONE

KYLA

Of course, of all places, he wants to go to Whiskey Barrel.

I puff my lips out and release a slow exhale. Rain trickles down the window, my breath fogging the glass. A lump I've been struggling to swallow is forming in my throat.

The news reported a tropical storm hitting the East Coast, but we're only expecting to get hit with the outer bands. It's symbolic of the absolute hell of a week I've endured with finals consuming my life.

I've graduated with my college degree, so my father can finally get off my back.

He gave up on riding my older brother, Madden, a long time ago. I guess when your son is the drummer for one of the biggest rock bands on the radio, you start to let shit slide.

Warm skin brushes over my thigh, and I shift my gaze over to Canon. He tangles our fingers together, lifting our joined hands to press a soft kiss against the back of mine.

A pair of black Ray-Bans hides his eyes, despite the sun being nowhere in sight.

My gaze snaps down to his mouth when he drags his lip between his teeth. He's dressed in a black T-shirt and denim jeans, fitting him perfectly in all the right ways. His tattooed arm is stretched out, his tanned hand firmly gripping the steering wheel. He looks every bit of the rugged badass your parents want you to stay far away from.

Except my parents love him, even if it's only because of his last name.

"It's a Friday night. Wouldn't you rather take me back to your place and fuck me against the wall?"

He slides his sunglasses off and curls the edge of his lip in a smirk. His eyes narrow, and for a second, I think I may have got to him.

He whips the car into a spot in the parking lot. He reaches for the lever to the door, then glances back before pushing it open and stepping outside.

"Dammit." I huff.

My heart drops to the pit of my stomach as the door shuts. Not because of the rejection.

It's the last thing I'd ever expect from Canon. He's never given me a reason to doubt him or his love for me since we started dating last summer.

No, the twist in my stomach has everything to do with the fact I'm only a few minutes away from seeing Tysin.

Tysin Briggs is the biggest player in Carolina Beach and a recipe for heartbreak. Yet it didn't stop me from falling in love with him two years ago. The rush and the high were intoxicating, but the crash coming down left me broken in a million pieces.

The day I walked out of the hospital, I vowed to stay as far away from him as I could. We've managed to avoid each other, but I knew this day would come sooner or later.

He's my brother's best friend and bandmate. We live in the same small town. Whiskey Barrel was his hangout, where the band started out playing all their shows.

There would be no avoiding him here.

It wasn't until Canon came along that I finally began putting the pieces of my heart back together.

My relationship with Tysin, if you could even call it one, was always kept a secret. Somehow, that made it even harder to move on.

If it weren't for the memories that haunted me and the ache in my chest, I would've thought it was all a dream.

"You comin' or what?" Canon teases, snapping me from my thoughts when he opens my door.

I climb out, stepping to the side to let him close the door before he stops me, pushing me against the side of the car.

All the stress and anxiety melt away when he pulls me into him, and I slip my arms around his waist. He trails his lips from my temple, where he presses a kiss, down to my ear.

"Let's have some fun tonight, yeah? I mean, you did just graduate from college. You should be fuckin' excited, baby. You did it!"

Guilt pangs in my chest. Why am I letting thoughts of running into Tysin ruin my night when I have Canon right in front of me?

"I always have fun when I'm with you."

He grins, tilting his forehead against mine, and kisses me deeply. I slide my fingers over his chest and pull him down, gripping the back of his neck to hold him to me. He moans, the move vibrating against my hand.

"Let's go have some fun. You deserve it."

He reaches for my hand, lacing our fingers together while we walk through the parking lot. There's a shift in my mood, a noticeable weight lifting from my chest as we round the corner toward the bar. A long line wraps around the front of the building, which only happens on the nights when A Rebels Havoc plays.

"Isn't that Tysin?" Canon asks, motioning toward the side of the building.

I follow his line of sight, my eyes immediately locking on Tysin. He's leaning against the wall, his foot tucked under him.

So much has changed since the last time I saw him. Even the way he stares at me now. The once heated look of desire is now replaced with a bitter coldness.

I know, without a doubt, he sees me, his eyes falling on where our hands are linked together.

I grit my teeth, knowing it won't be as easy to avoid him as I hoped.

He lifts his cigarette to his mouth, taking a deep inhale. His eyes eventually drag from me over to Canon before releasing a slow puff of smoke.

He's wearing a pair of black denim jeans and a red T-shirt with matching scuffed-up Vans.

I hate him for how deliciously sexy he still is, even after all this time.

It dawns on me that Canon asked me a question. Turning to find his eyes burning into the side of my face, I nod, responding with a clipped, "Yep."

When I turn my gaze forward, I notice Tysin's eyes are back on me, slowly raking over my body.

The bouncer near the front recognizes me and nods, waving me past him.

"Didn't expect to see you tonight." Tysin's deep voice grumbles as we pass by. "I thought I ran you out of here a long time ago."

My footsteps falter, and it takes everything in me not to give him a piece of my mind. It's what he wants, though. If I let him get under my skin, and he knew how much it bothers me, we'd be back to the same old cat and mouse games he likes to play.

"What was that about?" Canon questions. He looks at me, then back over at him, his brows deepening in confusion.

"Who knows?" I reply, trying to brush him off.

Meanwhile, the lump forming in my throat grows, making it impossible to ignore.

Whiskey Barrel is packed wall to wall with people. I overhear one of the bouncers tell Canon they've hit capacity, meaning they can't let anyone else enter. Carolina Beach has always turned up for their hometown heroes, and to this town, the guys of A Rebels Havoc are like gods.

It's exactly why I want to get out of here.

Canon's hand finds mine again as we make our way through the crowd of people toward the bar. The band always reserves the first couple of tables near the front. They loved the attention they got here and liked being able to mingle with the crowd.

The farther we get inside, I'm able to spot Brix and Ivy standing near the stage, and Madden isn't too far from them. He's built like a linebacker and is impossible to miss.

When we were in high school, the coaches didn't stop hounding him to join the team. He never had any interest in sports. At least not playing. His passion has always been music. Even when we were younger, he would turn anything and everything into a set of drums.

"You're here," Ivy cheers when the crowd parts. She crashes into me, pulling me into a hug.

Ivy's been my best friend since our days back in middle school. She always has my back, and I'll always have hers. When I found out Brix, her boyfriend and the lead singer, had made a bet with Tysin, I made it my mission to torture him.

He came to his senses and fought through hell to win her back, but she didn't make it easy on him, that's for sure.

Ivy was offered a job at *Mayhem Magazine* right after college. It's perfect for her since they're allowing her to travel with Brix on the road during the band's tour.

She will have the chance to do what she loves while also supporting his dream.

Their tour, Wreak Some Havoc, is big for them. Not only because they're headlining for the first time but also because most of their shows have sold out.

"I wish you were coming out on the road with me," she mutters against my ear. "What am I gonna do stuck on a bus full of smelly guys for three months?"

She pulls back, wearing a beaming smile on her face.

"You'll have to meet up with us at some of their shows, though. It'll be fun."

Madden sneaks in. "Congratulations, sis." He grunts, pulling me into a side hug. I practically disappear under his muscular arm.

The contrast between the two of us is almost laughable. He stands over a foot taller than me with arms the size of my head.

He slings his arm around my shoulders, pretending to put me in a chokehold. I playfully elbow him in the side before he finally releases me.

"All right, all right." He pushes me back. "Be careful before you take me out and I'm not able to have kids of my own one day."

"Lord help us all," I joke, shaking my head.

"Yo, Madden!" Brix hollers from a few feet away, nodding toward the stage.

"I'm gonna get stuff set up real quick, then I'll be back." He claps me on the shoulder. "I'm proud of you. At least one of us went to college. Pops can be happy with that, right?"

He chuckles, flashing me a wink as he backs away from us and turns to head toward the stage with the guys.

I notice the new guy Madden told me about is tuning his guitar, nodding his head along to the music. Tysin, thankfully, is nowhere in sight.

Canon comes up behind me, wrapping his arm around my waist.

"I'm goin' to grab us some drinks. I'll be right back."

I nod, running my hand over his forearm, and tilt my head up to give him a quick kiss before he disappears.

"I've missed having you at the shows with me," Ivy shouts. It's hard to hear over the music and the sounds of laughter and conversation booming around us.

If I'm being honest, I miss coming to them too. I love watching the guys play, even if it's different now.

"I do too," I say. She wraps her arm around my shoulders, and we sway back and forth to Three Doors Down.

It's been a while since we've hung out, so we use the few minutes we have with just the two of us to catch up. She tells me about how her new job is going and about the tour. They are only a few days away from leaving.

I'm still waiting for the day when Brix proposes. It's only a matter of time before it happens, but they're enjoying their time just the two of them while they can.

"What about you?" She rests her head on her palm. "What's next for you?"

There's a smug look on her face, almost as if she's keeping a secret, and she's bursting at the seams to tell me.

She reaches her hand across the table between us, stopping me midsentence, and tilts her head, signaling to something behind me. When I glance over my shoulder, my eyes land on Canon.

I spin on my heels to face him when he drops to his knee in front of me. All the oxygen is sucked out of my lungs in one quick move.

The music stops, and the crowd turns to face us, the noise level dropping with them. I slap my hand over my mouth, my eyes widening as I stare down at him.

Everything moves in slow motion from there. He holds out the black box in his hand, wearing a beaming smile on his face. He turns his hat backward. Something about that melts me every time he does. The sight of him, kneeling in front of me with the happiness radiating off him, grabs ahold of me.

How could I not want to spend every day for the rest of my life with him?

The energy in the room shifts, urging me to look up. It's almost as if I could feel the heat of Tysin's gaze, but I immediately regret it the moment I do.

My eyes lock on his. His face, his expression, is unreadable. Stoic. Emotionless.

I shake myself out of those thoughts, turning my attention back to Canon. I take a step toward him and bend forward, unable to hear him over the loud cheers and yelps of excitement erupting around us.

"I love you," I whisper against his mouth.

When I pull back, he smiles and presses another quick kiss against my lips.

"Then marry me?"

When Ivy asked me what was next, this is what I want. Canon. He's my future and the person I want to spend my life with.

I may not have a job waiting for me or all the next steps figured out, but I know I want all of it with him.

"Yes." I grin, nodding enthusiastically.

When he stands and wraps his arms around me, his lips crash against mine in a hard kiss. When I close my eyes, letting myself soak in the moment, I see Tysin's face.

Nothing betrays you more than your own mind.

CHAPTER TWO

TYSIN

"Get your shit together, man!" I snarl.

We've been practicing for almost two hours, preparing for our tour. I'm already sick of this new kid.

A Rebels Havoc has had an incredible run for the past two years. We went out on the road last summer with High Octane, and it was the big break we needed. We had labels pounding down our door, wanting a chance to talk to us.

One approached us with an offer we simply couldn't refuse.

Except it came with terms, terms I wasn't too pleased with, like adding a second guitarist to our lineup.

I was ready to wave my middle finger in the air and tell them to stick their contract up their ass.

I didn't, though.

As much as it felt like a dick smack to the face, this is everything I've been dreaming of since I was thirteen years old. It was my final *fuck you* to my mom and everyone in Carolina Beach who ever doubted me.

My love for music and my determination to see us go big won out. If all I have to do is deal with him, I'll grit my teeth and sign on the dotted line.

I still hate how it feels like all my hard work, my dream, was being handed over to him on a silver platter. He doesn't have the respect to appreciate what he's been given.

"Chill out, man!" Brix grunts under his breath.

He notices me take a step toward Trey. Pushing between us, he shoves me on the chest, attempting to calm me down.

"Chill? How would you feel if after you spent hours on lyrics, perfecting your vocals, some kid came in and re-wrote them all?"

Brix understood. We were one and the same. Cut from the same damn cloth.

Madden, on the other hand, is the voice of reason. The calm to our chaos. Whereas I had no filter and zero tolerance for bullshit.

The tension and frustration thrum through me. Brix mutters under his breath to calm down. We're crowded into the small space of our practice studio. It's our second home, the place we've used all those years.

Only now, it's starting to feel like we're crammed into a pressure cooker.

One word and we're all about to explode.

"He's right," Brix says, agreeing with me. He turns, pushing his hand against my chest. His eyes bounce over to Trey, then back to me. "We've busted our ass for the past six months, so we don't need you comin' in here and changing shit right before we leave on tour."

Trey scoffs, rolling his eyes.

"Whatever you say." He holds his hands up, shaking his head. "I didn't realize when I joined that I was gonna be stripped of my balls too. If you want to keep playing out of rhythm, more power to ya."

"Maybe we should call it a day," Madden suggests from behind his drums. His shirt is drenched, and beads of sweat drip down his face.

"Good idea. Tysin needs to go home and take some fuckin' Midol," Brix quips, crossing the room to swipe his bottle of water.

Trey joins in, a smirk stretching across his face.

"Fuck you and you," I jest, pointing at both of them.

We were all in bad moods before we even rolled in here. The truth is, we don't have time to mess around. Our tour starts in less than a week. We came back home to enjoy some downtime before we hit the road.

I was fine with wrapping up for the day. Everything about the past twenty-four hours has me ready to hit Whiskey Barrel for a beer and find someone to take back to my place.

"I need to get home and shower. We have that thing over at your parents' at six," Brix says, taking a large gulp

My eyes bounce over to Madden's, confusion furrowing my brow.

"What thing?" This is the first I've heard of anything going on.

"His parents are throwing a surprise engagement party for Kyla and Canon."

Brix's gaze lingers on me for a moment, trying to gauge my reaction.

As if witnessing it wasn't enough, I saw pictures plastered all over social media this morning.

Yeah, we had a fling. It wasn't anything serious, but it hadn't ended well. Not to mention, she was livid when she found out about the bet between me and Brix and how it hurt Ivy in the process.

She made it clear how much she hates me. Which is fine with me. I don't have any plans to try to change her mind.

In fact, the more she hates me, the easier it is for us to stay the hell away from each other.

Everything about being in CB has me wishing I could leave on tour now. It's only a matter of time before my mom catches wind we're in town. She'll come sniffing around, looking for a handout like she always does. As soon as she heard about our record deal, she was blowing up my phone to the point I blocked her number.

If she thinks for a second I'm giving her a dime, she's outta her damn mind.

Living in LA allowed me to distance myself from this part of my life. I'm ready to hit the road and do the same. With everyone chirping about Kyla's engagement, it couldn't come soon enough.

"You can come by if you want," Madden adds.

He has no idea about my history with his sister. We all knew if he did, it wasn't gonna go over well. He made it clear growing up that dating his sister was off-limits.

Probably because he knew Brix and I weren't the relationship type.

Guess he was wrong about Brix.

It wasn't worth the fight anyway. I got what I wanted out of our time together. The past is better left in the past.

"Nah, man. I think I'm gonna head home, have a few beers, and call it a night."

Madden stands, reaching into his pocket, and pulls out his phone. His brow furrows, a frown appearing on his face at whoever's calling. Brix and Trey are too busy talking about one of the songs we practiced today to notice.

He waves his hand at them, motioning with his finger over his mouth to be quiet before he answers the call.

"Hey, Harper, we're doing good. We just wrapped up a practice session now."

"Yeah, they're all still here. What's going on?"

What the hell is the owner of the record label calling Madden for? Especially so close to the start of our tour.

I pick up on the panic laced in his words, putting me on edge. My eyes bounce from Madden over to Brix. He steps away from Trey, folding his arms and tilting his head forward to listen in.

Madden nods, running his hand over his jaw, his gaze burning holes into my hardwood floors.

"What does this mean on such short notice?" he asks.

Brix flicks his eyes over to me, and I grit my teeth.

"Well, I think I know someone who could help us out. I'd have to talk to her. It's my sister. She graduated from college earlier this month with a degree in business management. While she doesn't have experience in managing a tour, she's been around the band since we started. She knows the ins and outs of what goes on behind the scenes. Plus, I trust her."

What the fuck is he talking about?

"Yeah, I'll see her here in an hour or so. I'll talk to her about it then. What is our backup plan if this doesn't pan out?"

His eyes widen, and he nods his head. I don't want to know her response but judging by the concern on his face, it's not good.

"We'll figure it out. We'll make it happen."

His words were confident and reassuring, but I know Madden. The dread on his face and the tension coiling in his body is anything but relaxed.

He ends the call, and his shoulders slouch in a heavy sigh.

"What was that all about?" Brix asks.

"The tour manager they hired fell through. Family emergency. We're less than a week away, making it hard to find a replacement."

"What's that fuckin' mean?" Brix barks, voicing what we're all thinking.

"She couldn't say, just wanted to let us know. I told her I'd talk to Kyla. She's the only person I could think of who could help us on short notice."

Madden scrubs his hand over his face, and my body goes rigid at the thought.

Three months stuck on a tour bus with Kyla?

Someone hand me a fuckin' beer now because I'm gonna need it.

CHAPTER THREE

KYLA

"It's only three months," I whisper to myself.

Those were the words I've recited over and over since Madden offered me the job. I was joining A Rebels Havoc as their manager for their summer tour.

If I'm being honest, I'm not ready to be crammed on the bus with four loud and rowdy guys. Especially one who I had a secret relationship with two years ago. It doesn't matter, though, because I need a job and money.

I could hear my dad's snide comments about my career choices running through my head on an endless loop. I didn't want Canon or his family to think I was only with him for his money.

Canon comes from one of the most prominent families in Carolina Beach. He and his brother, Cove, grew up racing motocross professionally. Their father owns the largest Powersports dealership in the state.

The Watt name comes with a level of expectation and notoriety I'm pressured to live up to when marrying him. Despite Canon reassuring me not to worry about money, sparing no cost when it comes to our wedding, something doesn't sit well with me by expecting him and his family to foot the bill.

I want to make something of myself and prove it to my family and his.

My father made the same comments to Madden about the band when he kicked them out of our family garage back in high school. He didn't think they'd make it this far, yet look where they are now, about to board a bus for their first headlining tour.

This is their moment to play for thousands of fans and a chance for them to prove to their label they are more than a risk.

When Madden came to me, asking for a favor to come out on the road with them, I couldn't pass up the offer. The guys need my help, and I owe my brother the favor. Truth be told, they're helping me too.

Everything is coming together perfectly, except for the small detail of being forced to deal with Tysin for the summer.

I can't exactly call him my ex-boyfriend. Ex-fling, ex-hookup, ex-anything.

Maybe more like friends-with-benefits, although I'd hesitate to think he'd even consider us friends at all.

He's Madden's friend, not mine.

It doesn't matter anymore, though, because we've both moved on with our lives.

I'm determined to get through the tour without letting the past get between us.

"It's only three months, right?" Canon murmurs against my temple when he pulls me into his arms. We've both been repeating the same words to each other since I broke the news to him.

I nod, tilting my head back to stare up at him.

"We'll both be so busy, it'll fly right by."

Canon lives and breathes motocross. His summers are devoted to racing. If he's not on the track or in the shop working on his bike, he's on the road traveling to his next race.

"It is, but it'll still be the longest we've been apart from each other." I squint my eyes against the sunlight to meet his.

He forces a smile, one that doesn't reach his eyes, and nods. He's putting on a strong front, but even I see how hard it is for him to watch me go. We don't know how soon he'll be able to meet up with me on the road.

As confident as he is in us, I don't doubt he dislikes the thought of me on a bus all summer with a group of guys, even if one of them is my brother. If he did, though, he'd never voice it out loud. He's selfless, always putting my thoughts and feelings first, and I couldn't be more thankful for it.

I squeeze my arms around his waist, taking a second to close my eyes and inhale his clean scent.

"I'm going to miss you." He tucks his head against the side of my face, his breath fluttering against my ear.

I glide my hands over his chest and lace my fingers around his neck, pulling him closer to kiss me. His hands grip my hips, and I get lost in his touch.

"I'll miss you too." I smile when we break away from the kiss. "We have FaceTime. I'll call you every night, and we can text often. You'll be off winning all your races, and you won't even know I'm gone."

He shakes his head. "Not a chance in hell." He grins, lifting his hand to trace his thumb down the slope of my jaw, raising my chin for another kiss.

A horn honks from behind me, jolting me from our intimate moment. I fold my hand over my chest and suck in a sharp breath, attempting to calm my racing heart.

I spin around and my eyes land on Tysin pulling up in his souped-up black Cutlass. His eyes bore into me, dead and emotionless. He raises his hand from the steering wheel, flicking his fingers to motion for me to move.

There's more than enough room for him to pass by us. Not to Tysin, though. He wants to be an asshole for the sake of being an asshole.

I sweep my hand out, gesturing to the empty space. "You can go, jackass." I curl my lip.

Canon bands his arm around my waist, pulling me against his front.

"Hey, hey. It's not worth getting all riled up over," Canon reassures me.

I make sure to throw a glare Tysin's way as he drives past, staring blankly at me before pulling into Brix's driveway.

"What's with him?" Canon asks, dropping his arm from my waist. His face scans over mine, taking in the tension rolling off me, and I shake my head.

How do I explain to Canon my feelings for Tysin?

You're engaged, Kyla. You shouldn't have any feelings toward him at all.

Canon and Tysin are as opposite as night and day. Tysin is selfish and never took anything in life seriously. Even when I thought he cared about me, it was all a lie.

All he cares about is the band and getting laid. Any heart he may show you is to benefit one of those two things. I was a fool to think I meant anything at all to him.

He never stopped to consider how I'd feel when the truth about the bet between Tysin and Brix came out, or when I walked in to find him with women draped over him. He threw me away without a care in the world.

Picking myself up off the floor in the months to follow was one of the hardest things I've ever gone through. Only two people in my life know the depths of darkness I lived through, and that's Madden and Ivy. Except only one of them knows the truth of who's behind it all.

I still have a lot of pent-up anger toward Tysin. I made a promise to myself when I took this job to reinforce the wall I built between us, using it to distance myself from him.

As much distance as you can have when living in a forty-five-foot bus with the man you once loved.

Tysin leans his body out the window, shouting at Brix, who points at the empty stall in the garage next to Brix's truck.

"Trey should be here in about five minutes, then we're headin' out." Madden glances over at me, raising his brows and signaling with his finger to wrap it up.

Why the hell am I doing this again?

"I'm starting to regret this decision."

Canon pulls me back in his arms, resting his chin on top of my head. We stand there, soaking in each other's embrace for those last few minutes together.

I've spent nearly every day with Canon since we started dating a year ago. Being away from each other for this long will be one of the first true tests of our relationship.

"After this, I'm never leaving you again. You're stuck with me." I snicker, wagging my brows.

“My kind of torture,” he jokes. He grips my chin between his fingers and kisses me. This time, we’re not interrupted, and I open my mouth to him.

“I’ll call you later when I crawl into bed,” I promise. “We can video chat every night so I’ll never have to fall asleep without you.”

He rakes his teeth over his bottom lip. My eyes lock on them before slowly trailing up to meet his ocean-blue eyes. I’ve seen the desire in their depths before, and it’s only making it harder for me to leave him.

“I love you,” I whisper before he brushes his mouth over mine.

“I love you more.”

I step back, dropping our locked hands, and reach for the handle of my bag. Tears well up in my eyes, and I blink through them, guiding my suitcase behind me toward the bus. I turn back to him once more, lifting my hand in a short wave as I watch him climb into his car.

He smiles back at me, and I quickly blow him a kiss.

When I turn back toward the bus, Tysin is leaning against the side near the door. His arms are crossed, and his eyes are glued to my chest. He makes a slow trail down my body before traveling back up to read the text printed on my shirt.

He smirks and shakes his head, mocking the words “my heart is on that track” printed on the front. I bought it to wear when I watch Canon race, with his number seventy-seven in a heart on the sleeve.

“You think you’re ready to live on the bus with us for the summer?” His lip curls.

“I grew up with the three of you hanging around our house all the time. What’s the difference?” I reply, face hard and attempting to appear as unamused as he is.

If you're close to Tysin, only then do you get to see his light-hearted side. I saw glimpses of it growing up over the years and during the summer we spent together.

The more I started to peel back the layers, the more I started to realize there's more to him, a lot I'm sure even Brix and Madden don't know.

I'll never forget when Tysin showed up at our house in the middle of the night when I was ten years old. It had been pouring rain all night. His hair and clothes were drenched from making the two-mile walk to our place.

Madden never got the full story from him. Not even my mom could when she pressed him on it the following morning. He moved in with his grandma shortly after it happened and a few months later she passed away.

"What about Pretty Boy over there? He okay with lettin' his girl loose for that long? The pout on his face sure says he ain't happy to give up his toys for long."

We've spent no more than ten minutes together, and he's already up to his bullshit. How could I have been so foolish to ever think I meant anything to him?

"Not all men view women as an object to fuck 'n' chuck, Tysin. He's not like *you*."

His eyes narrow, darkening, and he tilts his head down. I clench my jaw when he takes a step toward me.

"No, but I bet you wish he was." He rakes his teeth over his lower lip. "I bet you never stopped wishing it was me you were fuckin' too."

He's baiting me to see if he can get under my skin. I know him too well, though. I spent years watching him, soaking up everything about him when he was around.

He wants to provoke me to see how I'll react. The longer I play it off like I don't care, the sooner he'll learn to leave me the fuck alone.

He pretends to reach his hands out, mimicking him gripping a woman's hips before thrusting into her. My mouth opens before I quickly slam it shut, curling my lip in disgust.

I glance around for any sign that Madden and the guys are paying attention to us. Madden's in the garage, a phone pressed to his ear, and Brix is talking to an older guy who I believe is the bus driver.

When the coast is clear, I take a step into him, close enough to let my breast brush against his arms now crossed at his chest. He clenches his jaw when I do, his gaze flashing from my chest back up to meet mine.

"He's nothing like you, and that's exactly why I'm with him."

CHAPTER FOUR

TYSIN

"The hell is your problem, man?" Madden grumbles.

"What do you mean, what is my problem? We're all standing around ready to go, and this dude is nowhere to be found."

I toss my suitcase beneath the bus and slip my sunglasses on to cover my eyes. Everything about today is starting to grind on my fuckin' nerves.

"It's not like he intentionally took the wrong exit. He'll be here any minute," Madden retorts.

Trey's not from Carolina Beach. When we opted to spend our last week before our tour back home, he agreed to rent a place nearby so we could spend time practicing before we hit the road.

No more than a second after the words pass Madden's lips does Trey pull into the driveway. Brix motions for him to pull into his garage.

I catch Kyla's gaze when I do, standing across the driveway talking to Ivy. She notices me looking in her direction and turns her back toward me.

We all knew Brix would be dragging Ivy along on tour with us. The two are practically conjoined at the hip since they got back together. Although we tolerate each other, she's not a fan of mine after the bet that tore them apart.

Not only will I be forced to live next to Trey, who is beginning to fester under my skin, but I'll be stuck with Kyla and Ivy too.

This is nothing like I pictured our first tour going.

With her back facing me, I take a moment when no one is watching to soak in every inch of Kyla. It was hard to do the night of her engagement. As difficult as it is to know she belongs to him now, her long, dark brown hair reminds me of the last night we spent together.

Gone was the lavender-haired girl, struttin' down the boardwalk in her bikini and cherry-red lipstick. Those memories and the sight of her full lips wrapped around my dick still make me weak in the knees.

I've seen her around a couple of times at shows and on social media, but we've always managed to keep our distance. The last thing I've ever wanted or needed is Madden finding out what happened between us.

If he knew the truth, there's no telling how he'd handle it.

He has about forty pounds of pure muscle on me. He's built like a damn lumberjack. He's fiercely loyal and is protective of the people he cares about. If you cross him, you'll live to regret it.

"All right," Madden hollers. "Let's rock 'n' roll."

Our record label gave us the hookup with our bus. This bad boy only has a few hundred miles on it. Brix and Ivy claimed the king-sized bed in the back. There are two bunk beds open and a loft area above them. Madden and Trey take the beds in the loft, leaving Kyla and me to sort out who will take which bunk.

"I'm taller than you." I motion to Trey. "Why am I being left to this small-ass bunk?" I grunt, tossing my sunglasses on the table.

He runs his hand over his beard and smirks, shaking his head.

"They're the same," Trey quips, taking a seat on the couch. Madden sits in the chair next to him and flips on the TV.

"I'll take this one," Kyla interjects, pointing at the lower bunk.

We're left alone, the two of us. She folds her arms over her chest, waiting for my answer. She brushes her thumb over her lip, and the move draws my attention. She notices and stops, dropping her arms to her sides.

"It'll be me on top of you. Just like old times."

She flicks her eyes over to Madden, who's too focused on scrolling through the channels to notice.

"In your fuckin' dreams," she sneers.

I smirk, loving the fact I'm digging in under her skin the way she does mine.

"You're right. It's been a highlight of my dreams a few times, actually." The memories of pounding into her the last night have been front and center on my mind too many times to count when I've needed to rub one out. "It's too bad you've got a ring on your finger now."

She rolls her eyes. "You're disgusting. Not again, not ever. I'm the happiest I've ever been with the man of my dreams. You, on the other hand? I've heard all about where you've been getting your dick wet."

"Sounds like someone's been keeping tabs on me."

She scoffs. "Hardly. Your name gets around just as much as you do. Who would want to be with a man like you?"

Kyla tosses her bag on the floor next to her bunk. Her back is turned to me, and I take the brief second to myself to squeeze my eyes shut and shake my head.

I flex my finger and flatten my lips together, attempting to shake the emotions hitting me.

She has no idea how one simple question could land like a sucker punch to the gut.

No one will ever love you.

I stalk into the kitchen and lean against the counter.

"What the hell is your problem?" Madden quips.

We've been butting heads the last few days since Trey joined us.

Of course, he doesn't have a problem with him coming on board. It's not like they're adding a second drummer. Hell, I don't even mind that they want to add a second guitarist.

Why him, though? Somethin' about him was rubbing me wrong.

"Don't start in on me already," I snap. Opening the fridge, I swipe a container of orange juice. I sense Kyla's eyes burning into my skin when I open the carton and take a swig.

"You do realize there are other people on this bus, right? You can't just drink from the container." She shakes her head, moving to claim a spot on the couch next to Trey.

I swipe my mouth with the back of my hand, slamming the door shut, never taking my eyes off hers.

"C'mon, man. Knock it off, will ya?" Brix chimes in.

Meanwhile, Trey stares back and forth between us with a smug look as if he doesn't have a care in the world.

Why would he? He didn't have to bust his ass for years to get the band where we are today.

I tried to reason with our label managers that we didn't need him joining and even suggested some other guys who would kill it and mesh well with the rest of us. It fell on deaf ears.

They didn't give a shit. Their response was to figure it out and make it work.

Ignoring them, I stalk toward the front of the bus and take a seat across from Kyla. She's dressed in a pair of black shorts, showing off her tan skin. She's added a new tattoo since I last saw her, spanning the length of her thigh, and fuck me if it's not hard to stare.

She flips her hair over her shoulder and presses her lips together. It's written on her face clear as day that she's got something on her mind, but she's holding back.

"If you got somethin' to say, spit it out," I grumble.

"I'm not doing this with you, Tysin," she mutters.

"You didn't have a problem speakin' your mind two minutes ago." I relax my arm across the back of the couch.

"You're just ..." She shakes her head as though she doesn't want to bother finishing the sentence. "You're rude. That's what you are."

"Do you think I care what the fuck you think of me, Kyla?"

She chuckles, seemingly baffled by my question.

"I'm done talking to you."

Trey chuckles. "This is gonna make for an interesting summer, huh?"

I narrow my eyes on him, watching his gaze bounce between the two of us as if he's trying to dissect our relationship.

Kyla pulls her phone out and begins typing away. I start imagining some sugary-sweet message she sends off to Pretty Boy with hearts and flowers, gushing over how much she misses her perfect fiancé.

Gag me.

She reaches into her pocket, pulls out her earbuds, and swipes the screen to answer a call.

"Hey, babe," she croons, her voice changing from the condescending tone she had a moment ago.

I roll my eyes. Is this what I'll have to deal with during the whole tour?

I don't know what she sees in this dude other than dollar signs. Canon Watt came from money. His older brother, Cove, was in the same grade as Madden and me. He always thought his shit didn't stink.

"We're just about to Virginia," she says.

We left town early to get a head start on our ten-hour trip to Philly. We have a radio interview tomorrow before our first show and wanted to make sure we had time to set up and practice before we got on stage.

"How'd your practice go?" she asks, draping one leg over the other.

I attempt to focus my attention on the TV, but it's futile. My gaze is stuck on her toned thigh and the mandala tattoo disappearing beneath her shorts. Flowers are etched around the shapes, shaded in black and gray.

No matter how good she looks, even after all this time, or how my body reacts when she's near, I can never go back down that road. Not only because she belongs to someone else now, but because we both know I was never good enough for her.

She deserves someone like Canon, who could play the role of the perfect husband and give her the family and life she's always wanted.

I could never be the man she deserves. I'm too damaged, too selfish, too fucked up.

I suck in a deep breath, shaking myself from my dark thoughts.

Trey chuckles under his breath. I narrow my eyes and curl my lip in a sneer. When he raises his brow and tilts his head to the side in a silent taunt, I know full well he caught me staring. His face says, "I could say one sentence and blow your cover right now."

"I've only been gone for a couple of hours." She giggles. "I can't right now, but maybe later tonight."

Her voice drops low, and my stomach churns at the insinuation of where this conversation will lead.

"Stop." Her cheeks turn a dusty shade of pink, matching the color of her supple lips.

Listening to their conversation and the sound of her voice is starting to grate on my nerves.

"Please tell me I don't have to listen to this shit for the next three months," I grunt.

Kyla's eyes dart over to meet mine.

"Hey, Tysin, why don't you sit quietly and hold this for me?" Kyla asks, and I tilt my head to the side.

She lifts her hand, raising her middle finger to flip me off.

Trey throws his head back laughing, which makes Kyla grin before going back to her conversation.

"You know, there's plenty of room for you to go elsewhere. You don't have to sit here and talk about that shit."

"You're gonna have to get used to it at some point, Tysin."

"What makes you think anyone wants to hear it, though?"

I glance at Trey, expecting to find him with a smug grin knowing I finally broke. He, Brix, and Madden are carrying on a conversation talking about last year's Twisted tour.

It looks like the coast is clear, and they aren't paying attention until Trey brushes his tattooed hand over his beard and smirks, shaking his head. His man bun on top of his head bounces. I want to grab him and beat him in the head with the throw pillow next to him.

I don't, though. Instead, I chuck it at him. He catches it. Only this time, he doesn't downplay his amusement.

"Aw, man. C'mon now. What's got you all in a twist?" He barks out a laugh.

Brix and Madden both shoot us a warning sneer.

"Shut the fuck up, man. We all know your time on this bus and with the band is short-lived. Go choke on a dick."

Kyla hangs up the phone and storms past me to sit at the table across from Ivy. It's taking everything in me not to continue my rampage, giving Trey a piece of my mind.

All I care about is getting the band to the top, and I'll stop at nothing to see it happen.

Even if it means stepping back and letting our label bring in a smug fucker like Trey to do what I'm capable of doing.

I may hate every second of it, but I'll bite my tongue because, in the end, they're helping push my dream.

It's still going to make for a long summer.

CHAPTER FIVE

KYLA

It doesn't take long for the reality of being cooped up on a bus with six people to sink in.

I grew up around the guys. It wasn't long ago I was living at home with Madden and saw firsthand the havoc they wreaked around town. They're loud and messy, and I learned to pick and choose my battles where that was concerned.

I've decided to do my best to steer clear of Tysin, especially when he's in his moods. We have a lot of time ahead of us, and there's no sense in making it more difficult this early on.

"Are you excited to start wedding planning?" Ivy gushes, folding her hands beneath her chin.

We're seated at the small dining table with our laptops open. I'm working through organizing everything for the guy's upcoming shows and haven't thought too much about it, aside from bringing a stack of wedding magazines with me to flip through during my downtime.

"Nothing serious yet. We've talked about venues, though. Canon's dad is on the board of directors for the country club. His parents want us to have it there."

The guys are bent over the coffee table between the two couches, jotting down notes on papers strewn about. They've been writing new music and brainstorming lyrics.

I hear the distinct sound of Tysin's laughter, and I glance over Ivy's shoulder to find him staring at us with a smirk on his face.

"Lucky for you, you're marrying into money. Right?" He tilts his head to the side.

Madden's head darts up, overhearing him, and he slugs Tysin on the arm.

"What the fuck's your problem?" Madden's nostrils flare, his jaw clenched.

Tysin holds his hands up in surrender and shrugs. "I'm just messing with her, man."

I roll my eyes and shake it off. Despite his condescending comments, I'm not letting him ruin my excitement.

"The whole country club feels too stuffy for me, though." I shrug. "I've talked to Canon about how I'd rather do something outside as the sun is starting to set."

Ivy's eyes light up. "Especially since your color is purple. It would be beautiful with the night sky behind you."

My face warms, and I smile. "I thought it would be so romantic with candles scattered around too."

Ivy sighs. "It really would."

I've always dreamed of falling in love and getting married, although I've never been traditional or stuck by societal norms.

"I forgot to tell you, though. Canon's mom was there when I brought up wanting a black wedding dress."

Ivy's eyes bulge before she bursts out laughing. "Oh God. I can only imagine the look on her face when you told her. How'd she take it?"

"Canon even agreed. We thought her head would spin out of control and roll right off her shoulders."

I fold my lips together to contain my laughter, but it's useless. I slap my hand over my mouth to try to hold it together.

"I need a fuckin' beer," Tysin bellows.

After setting his guitar on the stand, he stalks through the kitchen toward the fridge and throws the door open. Ivy rolls her eyes and mouths to me, "Ignore him." She's never forgiven Tysin for how he hurt me, on top of finding out about the bet.

Growing up, I always thought Tysin saw me as Madden's little sister and nothing more.

Until the day he walked into Breaking Waves, the small-town surf shop I worked at back home. We were alone, away from anyone else, and he let his guard down enough to show me I was wrong.

I spent the whole summer hoping he'd open up and see me as more than the girls he'd bring home with him from Whiskey Barrel. At one point, I thought he did, but I had been wrong.

So very wrong.

We went our separate ways. I've moved on and found a love I never knew existed. I can't let myself get lost in the memories or forget what I have waiting for me back home.

It still doesn't stop me from searching for glimpses of the man I thought he was when I see him, even though I know he's not there. The man I thought I loved is nothing like the man he's proven himself to be.

You don't hurt people you love the way he crushed me.

It was one of the hardest lessons I've ever had to learn.

Ivy's computer dings with a notification, and she turns her attention back to her screen, furiously typing away to whoever is on the other end.

I do my best to shut out the fact Tysin is standing a few feet away, practically looming over us. I notice him take a long swig of his beer out of the corner of my eye before he releases a heavy sigh.

I'm dressed in a tank top and black denim shorts. My leg is crossed under my butt, and the other bounces on the floor beneath the table. I set my phone down next to me, forcing myself to get back to work.

It's hard to focus when the intensity of his gaze burns into me.

"How much longer before we reach Philly? And where the fuck are we?" Tysin hollers.

"We're outside Baltimore now. We still have a couple of hours until we are there!" Hank shouts back.

Six hours into our trip and he hasn't stopped complaining.

"We have all night to get there and check into the hotel. Can we pull off somewhere and find something to eat, maybe hit up one of the bars?" Tysin asks.

Madden and Trey glance up from where they're working at the mention of a bar. I predict the next words out of their mouth will be convincing Hank to make the stop.

"You don't mind, do ya?" Tysin teases. "Can you add that to your little plan?"

He takes a step toward us, setting his arm down on the back of my seat, and points at the papers.

"It's getting a little stuffy in here. I need some food, a beer, and to get laid."

He chuckles under his breath, flashing me a wink, and my stomach churns. He has no regard for anyone or their feelings.

All he cares about is getting his dick wet, and he doesn't give a shit who it's with.

My lip curls and he smirks, clearly amused by my obvious disgust. This time, he doesn't disguise the look on his face when he drags his eyes over my body, pausing on my chest before trailing down my legs and back up to meet mine.

Ivy is too focused on her conversation to notice anything going on. Madden and Trey are both practicing their music, Madden on the practice drum pad and Trey on his guitar. Brix is nodding his head in time to the beat, scribbling in his notebook.

I turn back toward Tysin, and he bites his lip, shaking his head as if he's trying to restrain himself.

"I'll see what I can do to help you take care of your little problem."

I slide out of the booth seat, and he steps back. There's not much room to pass by, leaving me to push my shoulder into his chest when I walk past. He reaches for my arm, stopping me in my tracks, using his body to shield us from the rest of the bus.

I jolt my arm out of his grip and narrow my eyes at him. "Don't touch me."

"I'm sorry. Little problem?" He smirks.

I raise my brow and shrug. I'm not going to sit here and praise him or his junk.

"You haven't changed at all over the years, have you? Still going out, getting drunk, and sleeping with whoever is willing to crawl into your bed. I would've thought you'd outgrow this stage at some point." I roll my eyes.

"I'll never change who I am. Not for anyone or anything."

I snicker. "Oh, I know. You're still the same selfish asshole you were two years ago."

"I told you before, but I'm glad you finally learned for yourself."

He did tell me. I guess I wanted to believe that somewhere deep down, there was more to why he was the way he was. Like maybe one day, the wall he had up for everyone around him would come down. There were times I could've sworn I saw it with my own eyes.

He warned me I was wrong and cautioned me not to fall for him. Like the fool I was, it didn't stop me from wanting him. If anything, I only seemed to want him more.

His face softens, and I can't help but wonder if he's thinking back to those memories too.

"Leave me alone, Tysin," I warn, holding my hands up between us. "Just leave me alone."

He takes a step back, reaches for his beer, and takes another swig. When his gaze meets mine again, his face is blank. The closed-off Tysin is back, and his wall is up, his emotions locked securely in place.

He warned me he was no good for me and would only break my heart.

He had been telling me the truth all along.

CHAPTER SIX

KYLA

We were ready to get off the damn bus by the time we made it to Philly. Everyone could feel the tension brewing between Tysin and Trey, and it seemed to make Madden grumblier by the second.

Brix and Ivy snuck off to their room as soon as we checked into our hotel, wanting their time alone. I claimed the other room in their suite, leaving Tysin, Trey, and Madden to room together in the other suite.

The guys decided to hit the club after dropping their bags in their room. Standing outside their door the next morning, I release a heavy exhale and reach my hand up to knock. I hold my breath, not knowing what kind of disaster I could be walking into or what I could end up seeing.

They have to be up early for their radio interview. Who knows when they made it back or how much sleep they got.

I hear shouting on the other side of the door just before the lock clicks, and a sleepy Tysin pokes his head out.

"I wasn't expecting you to turn up at my door already. You do realize your brother is asleep in here too, right?"

A slow grin spreads across his face. He reaches his arm up, resting his elbow on the doorframe. I try not to stare at his muscles or the intricate detail of the tattoo covering the length of his arm down to the top of his hand. I do my best to ignore his perfectly chiseled abs sculpting his stomach.

His hair is messy, longer on top and shaved on the side. The disheveled look from sleeping made him even more handsome, and I don't doubt he knew it too.

I shouldn't be noticing these things about him. I try to remain unaffected, which is easy to do until he curves his mouth in a smirk, doing crazy things to my insides.

God, I fucking hate him.

"Not gonna happen." I shake my head, pushing the door open, and take a step to shoulder past him. "Stick to your dreams, rock star."

He steps in front of me to stop me and raises his brow. "I'm giving you shit." His voice changes, shifting from playful to serious. "It seems as though someone's forgotten who ended things between us."

"There never was an *us*," I retort. "It's something we can both be thankful for now. Right?"

He pushes off the doorway and stalks into the room. I quickly reach out to stop the door from closing on me.

"Everyone dressed?" I holler into the room. "We've gotta leave here in twenty minutes. I set a wake-up call for you. Didn't they call you?"

"They did. We just didn't listen."

I roll my eyes and notice both doors to the bedrooms are closed, and the pull-out bed is open with blankets strewn on top.

"Trey brought someone back with him last night. I think she's still here." He knocks on Trey's door before poking his head inside.

"We gotta leave here in twenty."

"Can you shut the fuckin' door for a second? I'm not even dressed," Trey bellows.

"Is your guest still here?" I ask Trey, staring at my phone to check the time.

"Yeah, she's in the bathroom. Can you order her an Uber to take her home for me?"

I nod. "Who am I calling it for? Please tell me you at least thought to ask for her name."

"As a matter of fact, I did. Her name is Mona."

I hear a door open, and a tall redhead appears in the doorway. Trey pulls her into his arms, kissing her. I turn away, giving them their privacy.

"Good luck at your show tonight." She smiles at Trey.

She's stunning, dressed in a cobalt-blue lace top and distressed black jeans. She's clutching a pair of high-heeled booties with a wristlet hanging from her arm. She quickly runs her hand through her hair to tame the strands.

"Thank you for the lift." She flashes me a warm smile and disappears out of the room.

I pound my hand on Madden's door next. I've learned the hard way it's impossible to wake him up unless you drag his ass out of bed. I swear, he could sleep through the sound of a freight train.

"Madden!" I shout, as the door swings open, scaring me.

"Can you just chill out?" he bellows. He drags his hand over his face and rubs the sleep from his eyes.

"You couldn't think to wake us up earlier? Why wait until the last fuckin' minute?" he grumbles.

"If you need me to call an Uber for anyone," I ask, glancing over his shoulder, "tell me because we need to leave soon."

"No one's here."

"What happened to the brunette from the night before?" Trey asks.

"Mona? No, we're just friends."

Mona?

"Wait, what did you say her name was?" I ask Madden.

"Mona. She's the chick interviewing us at the radio station today. I met her last year on the Twisted tour."

I turn, pointing toward Trey and over at the door. "I thought you said the girl I called an Uber for is named Mona?"

He nods. "It is."

Madden finishes his drink of water, takes a deep breath, and shakes his head.

"Nah, man, that's not fuckin' Mona. The chick you left with last night is her cousin, River. No, wait, shit. Her name is Layken."

Trey's face falls, and he bends down, staring at the floor. I release a slow whistle and hold my hands up, stepping back.

"I'm gonna go get my suitcase from my room, and I'll meet you downstairs in the lobby in twenty."

Tysin stops and turns back to look at me once more. His face is blank with a T-shirt in his hand. He eyes me for a moment before he pulls the material over his head.

Our conversation stays on my mind on my way back to my room and downstairs. I take a seat in the lobby area, using the few minutes of peace to text Canon good morning and respond to a few emails.

The road crew passes through the lobby on the way to the arena to set up for the show. By the time we wrap up the interview, we should make it right on time for sound check.

The trip to the radio station is relatively quiet and doesn't take as long as expected. I chalk the somber moods up to the late night and lack of sleep. They're able to turn it on and wake up as soon as we arrive at the station, and they sit down for the interview.

I stand outside the sound booth, listening in with Ivy.

"Thanks for stopping by to hang out with us," Mona croons.

The other host, Austen, chimes in, thanking them too. "We're looking forward to your concert tonight. It's gonna be an epic show."

Brix, being the front man for the band, answered most of the questions. Although I didn't miss the not-so-subtle way Mona kept batting her lashes at them, especially Tysin, who claimed the seat closest to her.

I caught his gaze eyeing her chest and how he practically drooled over her legs when she crossed one over the other, hiking up her skirt.

She seemed to notice it too, flashing him a knowing smirk.

I hate that it even bothers me at all. I've been to plenty of shows and seen countless women throw themselves at the guys. They practically beg for their attention.

The guys play it off well and act like they don't even notice. Trey has been in a gloomy mood since the name mix-up earlier this morning. You'd think it wouldn't bother him so much for a one-night stand. I don't think he expects to see her again, but I guess I don't know him well enough either way.

I slip past Ivy into the hallway and pull out my phone. Security is standing outside the entrance. Abel nods his head in greeting as I walk past, click the call button, and lean against the wall.

When Canon's raspy voice filters through the line, a wave of calmness washes over me.

"I wasn't expecting to hear from you until later."

"Yeah, we're still at the radio station. The guys are doing their interview right now, so I thought I'd sneak away to call you. What are you up to?"

"I just got to the shop a little bit ago. I'm about to suit up and take the bike out for some laps before it rains."

We both knew we'd be busy and would need to take advantage of any time we had to catch up with each other. I'm hoping it'll get easier as time goes on.

He has a race this weekend and is feeling the pressure to start the season strong. Anytime he's stressed or nervous, it helps him to go for a ride to clear his mind.

The door opens to the lobby at the station, and the guy's loud voices filter out into the hallway. Madden signals for me to come back in, and I nod, holding my finger up to let him know I'll be there in a minute.

"They just wrapped up their interview so we're gonna head over to the venue now. I'll text you later when I can. Good luck, baby. I love you."

I ended the call and stepped back through the doors. Tysin is leaning against the wall across from me near the bay of elevators. He rolls his eyes, a smug smile on his face. I suspect he heard the end of my call, but who knows with him.

"We're staying in town tonight, right?" Trey asks.

I nod. "Our next show is about three hours from here in Jersey."

"Abel, will you tell the rest of security if a redhead named Layken asks for me to let her back to my dressing room? Please."

He nods, motioning for us to get into the elevator. I stand in the back next to Trey.

"You okay?" I whisper to him.

His eyes grow distant, lost in thought, and he nods. "If you see her there, will you let me know?"

"Of course." I grab his forearm, giving it a squeeze. "She was in the bathroom when you told me her name, Trey. She probably didn't even hear you."

He nods. "I don't know. She acted different this morning. Distant."

"Maybe she was just nervous. You met her at the club, right? Maybe it was the liquid courage."

"Yeah, maybe."

There's a crowd outside the station, so Abel calls through his wrist mic to have Hank pull around front.

"It's packed out there. I want you to go straight to the car, no funny business." He looks directly at Tysin, and he laughs.

I tune out their conversation on the way to the venue, scrolling through emails and messages from the crew. There's a mess to sort through with the lighting setup. We knew something would come up. It was bound to happen. I close my eyes and take a deep breath, reminding myself it'll all work out. Calvin, the crew manager, messaged me and told me they're on it and will make sure it's good to go before the guys take the stage tonight.

"If your girl comes by again tonight, tell her to bring Mona with her." Tysin sighs. "I'm ready for the after-party, if you know what I mean."

Why does it feel like he's determined to rub his sex-capades in my face?

Ivy peers at me out of the corner of her eye, checking to see how I'm handling his comments.

I don't care. If he wants to sleep with a new woman in every city we stop in, more power to him. I'd prefer he left me alone, and we stayed out of each other's business.

"There's gonna be a long line of beautiful women waiting for us in VIP too," Madden adds.

"You keep that shit up, and you'll have shit growin' off you," Ivy quips.

It was only a matter of time before she told Tysin off.

He's reclined back in his seat, and he moves his arm from where it's folded over his face, his eyes narrowing on Ivy. The sass she throws at him screams for him to test her.

"Unless I've got my dick inside you, you don't have shit to be worryin' about."

She clenches her jaw, her eyes finding me. She wants to say so much more, but she won't. Ivy would never betray me. She's loyal and knows it would be like throwing a live grenade in this van. Madden would go off like a ticking time bomb.

Only Madden and Ivy know the truth about the pain I was left with after our relationship ended. Except no matter how many times he asked, I never told Madden who I had been with. It didn't stop him from being there next to me, supporting me every step of the way.

If he knew it was Tysin, their relationship would never recover. I'm almost positive of it.

"Stop it with the fighting, both of you. You can't get along to save your life. Can we have ten minutes without bickering?" Brix snarls.

Tysin laughs, which only seems to piss Brix off more.

Ivy's face falls, clenching her jaw. Brix reaches for her hand, his face softening in apology. She yanks her hand away, and he moves his to caress her thigh instead.

"When have you ever known me to be quiet?" Ivy smirks.

Brix smiles and shakes his head. "Never, baby."

We all knew she'd find a way to get back at him for it too.

CHAPTER SEVEN

KYLA

"C'mon, it's go time!" I bang on the metal door and shout into the dressing room.

We arrived at the arena in Boston an hour ago. As busy as it keeps me, I live for it, especially after another long morning stuck on the bus.

I'm dressed in a black lace tank top with "I'm with the Rebels" printed on the front, a pair of denim jeans, and black Converse. It's hotter than a sonofabitch, so I opt to pull my hair up in a high ponytail with strands down framing my face.

"You can come in, ya know. It's not like you haven't seen me naked," Tysin bellows.

I slouch against the doorframe and roll my eyes, scanning my to-do list before checking the time on my phone.

There are three unread messages from Canon. My fingers itch to open them, but I don't have the time to respond, and I don't want him to think I left him on read either.

"Five minutes," I shout. "Hurry up."

I glance up as Madden rounds the corner, dressed in jeans and a graphic T-shirt. I smirk, reading the text, "You'd be loud if I was banging you too."

Trey follows him. His hair is down. It's the first time I've seen him without it pulled up. I'm envious of the strawberry-blond locks. Women would kill for hair like his.

"You can pull it if you want." He winks when he notices me eyeing his hair.

Madden smacks him on the chest and shakes his head. "Tysin may talk about kickin' your ass, but I'll actually do it."

I roll my eyes. "Is Brix coming?"

Madden shakes his head and laughs. "Interesting choice of words."

"What's that mean?" I ask.

Trey grins. "He walked in on Brix and Ivy goin' to town in his dressing room. I guess Brix was butt naked."

"He knows we have the meet and greet soon, right?"

"Oh, he knows. He said he's coming, but now that I think about it, I don't know in what context."

Trey and Madden burst out laughing. They're like a bunch of horny teenagers who can't keep their hands off each other.

The door swings open to Tysin's dressing room, and he stalks past me. He has a bottle of vodka in one hand, nearly empty, and takes a long swig before pulling on his hat.

He screws on the cap and sets it on the counter, then reaches into his pocket and pulls out his pack of cigarettes.

His eyes are dark, staring down at the floor. He's been in a mood since we got here, and like always, I've done my best to avoid him.

"We have to get goin'," I urge, staring at Tysin, trying to gauge how drunk he is.

"I'm fuckin' comin'," Brix shouts down the hall, sauntering toward us. He's holding Ivy's hand.

She bites her lip, trying to fight off her coy smile.

"Alright, let's go." I wave my hand over my shoulder, motioning for them to follow me. They're like herding cats, I swear.

Some days, I feel like a glorified babysitter. I'm here for the money, though, because in the end, it'll give me the wedding of my dreams.

Don't get me wrong, I want the band to succeed, but I'm only on the road with them for me.

The guys follow me into the convention hall set up for the meet and greet. The arena staff took care of sectioning off the room, creating a line into the hallway for the attendees.

Tables with A Rebels Havoc merch are lined up across from them. Ivy helps me keep the line moving, chatting with fans about the show.

It takes everything in me to stay composed when I hear some of the shit women say about the guys while waiting to meet them.

Ivy passes by a group of women talking about all the things they'd do if they could get Brix alone. I caught the devious gleam in her eye.

"You're giving me so many ideas," she jokes.

The women's brows furrow in confusion. Ivy simply flashes her a wink, clearly having no idea who she is.

I overhear another woman saying she wants to swallow Tysin's babies. It sends me into a coughing fit, nearly choking on air.

"I can't believe some of the shit they say," Ivy grumbles under her breath. She folds her arms over her chest, staring as one woman approaches Brix wearing nothing but a lace bra and a pair of shorts.

She holds out a marker to Brix, gesturing to her chest and asking him to sign her.

Brix laughs, nodding his head toward Ivy. The girl's head swoops over, and she narrows her eyes on Ivy. Ivy greets her with a small wave and a polite smile.

Before they got together, he would be eating up the attention. Now? He only has eyes for Ivy.

"It's the same for Canon and the track bunnies."

"Yeah, I'm sure they come around," Ivy adds. "Anytime I've gone with you to see him race, he doesn't ever look in their direction. He only wants you."

"Still, it doesn't help knowing the temptation is there. Ya know?"

"You trust him, though, right?"

I nod. Is it getting to me because I'm seeing all the girls who chase after Tysin and the band, and it worries me about what happens with Canon when I'm not around?

Or is it because, in some way, I feel guilty because being near Tysin again has brought old feelings to the surface?

Maybe a little bit of both.

I force the thought out of my mind and reason with myself that the feelings are only resurfacing because of grieving the loss of Tysin twice.

If he knew the depth of how badly he hurt me, maybe he'd feel differently. At least I tell myself he might.

It doesn't matter, though. There's no point in reopening old wounds and telling him the truth, knowing it would only hurt him.

Although saying it would hurt him could be giving him too much credit. He never seemed to care about destroying me before.

After the guys snap photos, another group of women approaches. One of them makes a beeline for Tysin, showing off her crop top with “Sexy as Sin” written across her chest.

Fans have nicknamed him Sin for years, all the way back to their days playing in Whiskey Barrel every Friday.

My heart leaps when he eyes her, recognizing the desire on his face. He pulls her into a hug, his hands gripping her curves settling low on her hips.

His hat is on backward. Even with the distance separating us, I can still make out the grin fighting to break across his face when he catches me looking his way.

A knot coils tight in my stomach when she pulls her shirt down, exposing her cleavage, and asks him to sign her chest too.

We get through the line of VIPs, and the guys take off to change while I meet up with Calvin to make sure we’re ready to rock ’n’ roll for tonight.

Madden’s standing in the hallway with Trey, beers in hand, shooting the shit with Abel when I check in with them.

Trey takes the last swig of his beer, tossing the can into the recycling bin.

“I’m gonna go warm up before sound check.” Madden grunts. Abel follows him.

“I’ll go with ya,” Trey adds.

“I’ll grab the other two, and they’ll meet you there.”

“I wouldn’t go in there,” Trey warns, stopping in his tracks.

He points at Tysin’s dressing room, and Madden nods in agreeance.

“Why?” I hate asking.

Trey glances over at Madden, struggling between fighting the urge to apologize and finding the words to tell me.

“I just wouldn’t.”

He doesn't have to say it. He has someone in there with him. I wait until the guys disappear down the hall before I clutch my clipboard to my chest and pound my fist against the door, urging him to wrap it the fuck up.

A few seconds later, the door opens and the brunette from earlier ducks her head out, slipping past me. She attempts to fight off her beaming smile.

"Oh my God." Her hair is matted to her cheek still slick with sweat. She waves her hand, fanning herself.

"He's ... wow. That was amazing!"

"Get the fuck out of here!" I shout. "Or I'll have you removed from the venue."

She rears back, her jaw falling open in surprise.

"I'm not kidding. Go!"

She takes off down the hallway. Anger and frustration settle over me, causing heat to rise up my neck.

I push the door open and slam it shut behind me, tossing my clipboard on the chair and crossing my arms over my chest. Tysin doesn't look the least bit surprised to see me.

He pulls his pants over his hips, adjusting the waist before buttoning them.

"I didn't expect you to give in so easily. Especially when you know I just finished, but if you want to take a turn, take your top off, baby. I'll be ready to go for round two in no time."

"Are you fuckin' kidding me?" I stalk toward him, pushing the tip of my nail into his bare chest.

He smirks, tilting his head down toward me, not backing off or giving me an inch.

A voice in the back of my head shouts that I'm not supposed to let this bother me. My eyes are drawn to the way he adjusts his pants on his hips and the obvious bulge, getting off on my jealousy.

His eyes follow my line of sight, taking in his face.

How is it that we're already back to this after only a few days into the tour?

He takes a step closer, towering over me. When I step back, the edge of his mouth curves in a smug smile.

"You want to play these cat and mouse games, Kyla?"

"No, that's the fuckin' point. I don't want to play any games with you. Look at us. We're already back to the same shit."

He steps toward me again. When he notices I don't step back, he takes another until we're standing toe-to-toe. He dips his head down, letting his warm breath heat my skin as it brushes across my jawline.

"We're not back to the same shit." He breaks through the silence. "If we were, I'd have you on that counter with your legs spread open, eating that sweet pussy like I know you want it."

His words cause my breath to hitch.

"You like the sound of that, don't you? Is that why you're pissed off? Are you mad because I was fucking her, or are you mad because you wish I was fucking you?"

When I don't answer, he trails his nose over my cheek.

"Which one is it, Kyla?" he whispers.

I grit my teeth and shove him away.

"You need to get cleaned up. You have an hour until you go on stage, and you smell like a wet dog."

He throws his head back and cackles. The sound grinds on my nerves, and it takes everything in me not to push him again.

When he rolls his head back down to look at me, his stare is blank. He stalks toward me, but this time, he doesn't stop. I press my back against the cold cinder block wall, sending shivers over my heated skin.

"You have nowhere to go now, little mouse."

"I'm not doing this with you, Tysin." My chest heaves.

What did I ever see in him for all those years? He never gave a shit about me or my feelings. The way he's treated me since we left on tour is evidence of this.

"Can we agree to stay away from each other? I'll give you space, and you'll stay out of mine. Deal?"

"Under one condition," he mutters.

I raise my brow, waiting for him to elaborate.

"I don't want to listen to you and Pretty Boy. Stay out of my business, don't worry about who I'm fuckin', and keep me out of yours."

"Deal."

This was for the best anyway.

I expect him to take a step back, giving us the distance we both agreed to. His eyes roam over my face before landing on my lips.

He clenches his jaw, flaring his nostrils. Pressing his hand against the wall, he leans in close to me.

He takes a deep breath and sighs. His lips hover near my neck, and my heart is thrumming so fast I'm afraid it'll beat out of my chest.

I fight off the urge to grip the front of his shirt and pull him closer to me. I hate myself for letting the thought even enter my mind.

When he reaches out to trace the hem of my pants, my body trembles with the intensity of an earthquake.

After all this time, my body still knows the difference between his touch and anyone else's.

"Tysin," I whisper.

"Mm-hmm," he moans lightly.

"Tell me it's a deal."

He stands there, not moving, but the tension in the air shifts between us.

"Deal."

The word is pointed and spoken with conviction. He turns, swiping his hat off the chair, and storms out of the room, letting the door slam shut. I don't bother to stop him.

A deal is a deal, after all.

CHAPTER EIGHT

TYSIN

After the first weekend, we followed through on our word and kept our distance.

Well, as much space as you can have while being crammed on a bus together.

I try to avoid looking in her direction, and she's kept her comments about me to herself. Whenever my past escapades are mentioned, she excuses herself from the room.

The one time I gave in to the temptation and glanced over in her direction, Kyla's face was clouded with uneasiness.

The regret and guilt twist inside me when I'm forced to see her beaming smile when a text message or call comes through from Canon.

She's happy and deserves someone who can give her the world. Even though that person will never be me.

We're hardwired differently. I'll never be able to give her the life she wants.

The house, a family, with kids of our own.

Kyla grew up in a home with a protective brother and the love of her parents always watching over her. As much as I hate to admit it, Canon is better for her and can give her more than I can.

I grew up living a completely different life than they did. My dad cut out before I was born, and my mom didn't give two shits about me. She couldn't bother to make sure there was food on the table or that I made it to school on time with clean clothes.

I learned from an early age not to rely on other people, and the biggest mistake Kyla ever made was holding out hope she could depend on me.

Growing up, if I wasn't off with Brix or Madden, my mom was sticking me with anyone she could find to look after me or with my grandma for the night. She'd spend her night clutching the brown bottle, with men coming in and out of our house, sneaking back to her room.

After my grandma passed away, she left me a decent chunk of change. When the judge signed off on my emancipation, I had enough to take care of myself until I graduated.

All I've ever cared about was the guys and doing whatever it takes to get A Rebels Havoc to the next level.

I'd do anything to make sure I never end up back in the hellhole I grew up in.

I've buried my feelings for Kyla deep down with the pain and torment I've carried with me from my past.

I don't give a shit about the line of women who flock to us, doing anything to catch my attention. It's only sex to me. Once I get what I want, I'm done with them too.

The end of July rolls around. We've had nearly a month on the road under our belt.

We played a show last night in Charlotte, and I loved being back in front of a hometown crowd.

We have a short break before our next show in Cincinnati, so we decide to lay low and enjoy time at home. It was good to sleep in my own bed for a change, too.

Brix and Ivy took off to stay at their beach house in Myrtle Beach, while Madden and Trey took off to God knows where.

When it's time for us all to board the bus again, we take off late in the evening, making most of the trip to Ohio overnight.

I don't bother standing outside, forcing myself to watch as Kyla says her goodbyes to Canon again. I climb onto the bus and crawl into my bed, passing out as soon as my head hits the pillow.

It's not long before I'm jolted awake, my insomnia making it impossible to get more than two hours of sleep at a time.

I reach under my pillow, searching for my phone to check the time, when I hear a subtle moan from the bunk below me. I squeeze my eyes shut, memories flooding me, forcing myself to believe it's coming from Brix and Ivy's room.

I'm tempted to put my earbuds in and blare music to drown them out when another low groan follows.

"Yessss," she hisses. "I'm so wet."

This time, the sound is unmistakable. I'd know that throaty voice anywhere, mixed with arousal dripping off her.

I grit my teeth, picturing her lying in her bunk, her legs spread open while she's touching herself. Only I know she isn't alone. There's someone on the receiving end of those words, and they aren't meant for me.

"I wish you were inside me."

I roll my eyes shut, letting myself believe she's talking to me.

My dick hardens, and I reach my hand beneath the waistband of my shorts, gripping my dick in my fist.

"I want your tongue licking my clit."

The visual of her thighs wrapped around my head causes my chest to heave. I pull my T-shirt up and bite down on the cotton material, attempting to cover up the sound of my heavy pants.

"Your tongue feels so fuckin' good," she moans. Her voice cracks, and it takes everything in me not to stop her right there.

We made a deal, and she's breaking it.

I stroke my dick, tightening my hand with each pump, gliding back down.

"Shiiiiitttt," I mutter.

I don't realize I said it out loud until I hear her breath hitch. Silence ticks by at an agonizingly slow pace before she whispers my name.

My dick ignores the panic in her voice. All I care about is she doesn't stop where this is going. I grit my teeth, squeezing the tip to fend off my release.

"No. I swear I heard Tysin," she whispers. "I thought he was asleep in the bunk above me."

I hold my breath, counting the seconds while I wait for her to continue.

"I did too," she fires off defensively.

I grin at the thought of him knowing his girl goes to sleep every night with me on top of her.

"I think he's asleep. He's snoring."

Now she's fuckin' with me because she didn't hear shit. She's quiet for another moment before her heavy exhale follows, and I roll my eyes shut at the sound.

"Fuucckk," she moans as the low hum kicks on.

It takes me a second to register the sound, but the obvious quiver in her voice and her quiet groans give it away.

The vibration increases, amping it up a notch, and I'm damn near ready to beg her to hang up the phone so I can help her finish.

"Do you like listening to me get off?"

I nearly choke on air, and my lip curls into a snarl as I grit my teeth. She's taunting me, playing it off like she's talking to Canon, but this is all for me.

"I wish I could watch you touch yourself for me," she continues.

I bet you fuckin' do, baby.

She's driving me crazy with need. Lying here, listening to her get off when I can't touch her, is pure fuckin' torture.

I adjust the waistband of my shorts over my hips to free my dick. I use my arm to cover my mouth, attempting to muffle any noise.

"I'm imagining you fucking me."

The humming changes, going from loud to quiet. It starts off slow at first, then grows faster as if timed perfectly with her heavy pants. I mimic her pace, squeezing my eyes shut to picture her legs wide while she slides her vibrator in and out, and I match her thrust for thrust.

"I'm close," she breathes out.

I clench my teeth, right there with her. I adjust my grip, sliding my hand over the tip, and brush my thumb over the head. The move spreads tingles throughout my body.

Sweat dots my brow, and my heavy breathing heats the small space.

I can't hold back anymore.

"I want you to come with me," she begs.

Her choppy words suck all the oxygen right out of me. I need her legs wrapped around my waist while she rides my dick until she milks me dry.

Nothing could prepare me for the sound of her throaty moan. Her mattress creaks, and I envision her trembling as the force of her release wracks through her body. Her breath hitching combined with her quiet, "Fuck," sends me over the edge.

I come so hard I expect my heart to beat out of my damn chest. It takes a few minutes before my heart rate returns to normal, floating down from the high.

"Tysin," she whispers, and I freeze.

Shit. She must've hung up with Pretty Boy.

"Go to sleep, Kyla."

"Are you going to pretend I didn't hear you?"

"You didn't hear shit. Go to sleep," I snap.

"Oh, so you didn't eavesdrop on my conversation with Canon, and I didn't hear you moan with me?"

"What happened to our deal?" I change the subject. "I shouldn't have to listen to this shit. My self-control only goes so far. If you don't want me to listen, you should save the conversation for when we hit the hotel tonight."

I shove my shirt down, my chest still slick with cum, and climb out of my bunk.

Her curtain is open, and I don't know what I'm doing, but clearly, I'm not thinking straight because I'm not prepared to see her.

Strands of her dark hair fall around her face, and her cheeks are stained pink under the heat of my gaze. Her nipples are hardened against the silky fabric of her top, causing my fingers to itch to pull the material down to touch her.

The thought makes me angry.

"Trust me." I grit my teeth, carefully whispering low enough so no one hears. "We both know if I still wanted you, it would've been me making you come. Don't lie. You know the only reason you got off is because you knew I was listening."

Her jaw drops, and she has the nerve to act hurt. "Are you kidding? You're a fuckin' asshole."

"You'll do well to remember it too. Now leave me the hell alone."

I clamp my mouth shut and stalk down the hall, stepping into the small bathroom and slamming the door shut.

She should've listened a long time ago when I told her to stay away from me.

CHAPTER TEN

KYLA

We're rolling in on two months since the tour began. The days seem to pass by in a blur, yet it feels like so much time has passed since Canon and I stood outside Brix's house saying our goodbyes.

We knew it'd be hard to be away from each other. This would be a test for us and our relationship, but I didn't expect it to be this difficult.

I slip the key in the lock and adjust my bag on my shoulder, pushing the door open. I don't bother bringing all my stuff in with me and just drop my suitcase, then kick off my shoes. I collapse on the mattress, tucking my legs under me, and pass out like a rock.

I wake a couple of hours later and check my phone to several messages from Ivy and one from Canon. My chest pangs growing tight with tension when I read his short message, one word, simply saying **Okay** when I asked him to call me tonight before he fell asleep.

Our schedules are busy, and it's starting to eat at me as the days turn to nights and I don't hear his voice before I fall asleep. Some mornings, I don't crawl into my bunk until after two in the morning.

Sometimes I'll have missed calls from Canon, but when I try to call him back, they almost always go unanswered.

I hate how distant we've become, and in the back of my mind is a niggling fear as to what this could mean for us. It's hard not to let the same fears from my relationship with Tysin creep in, even when I reason they're not the same.

Canon would never hurt me the way Tysin did. A cold knot twists in my stomach at the thought, and tears prick my eyes. We have our future mapped out together, and I don't know if I could handle losing Canon too.

My phone vibrates again with another text from Ivy.

Ivy: Are you alive? We're heading out to dinner in thirty minutes if you want to join us.

I giggle. We wrapped up our show in Kansas City the night before. With a much-needed break in our schedule, we decided to make the trip to Chicago overnight. As soon as we arrived early this morning, I warned Ivy and the guys not to wake me unless it was an emergency.

I fire off a reply to her and quickly pull myself out of bed, shaking my head when I catch a glimpse of my reflection in the mirror. Time for a shower.

We grab dinner at an Italian restaurant at the hotel, Vino's Ristorante. I sigh, covering my stomach with my hand, and take the last sip of my wine.

"Are you gonna come out with us?" Ivy asks, shifting her gaze from me over to the guys.

Trey and Madden chatted throughout dinner about hitting up Velvet, a local nightclub. Madden hasn't stopped talking about how sick he is of being cooped up, so I know without asking, he's already in the mood to hit the town.

Trey lifts his beer and mutters, "I'm in," clearly ready to head out with him.

"I'm in too." I nod as my phone pings with a text. The screen flashes with a number I don't recognize.

My number has been given out as a contact since the tour began, so it isn't uncommon for me to get various calls and messages. My job is to take the stress off the guys while we're on the road, so all the communication comes through me, keeping their focus on the tour.

The message is nothing but a link to a Wired Buzz article, causing my brows to deepen.

I recognize the name from an interview Canon did last year at the end of his racing season. I click on the link, and it pulls up an article, the headline reading, "Tensions heat as Watt climbs the leaderboard."

A video plays, and no more than ten seconds in, my heart sinks.

"Excuse me," I mutter, picking up the napkin from my lap and tossing it onto the table.

Madden's eyes dart over to me, picking up on the panic in my voice, and his face falls.

"What's wrong?" he asks.

"It's nothing. I just need to make a personal call."

He doesn't believe me. Judging by Ivy's face and the apprehension flickering in her gaze, she doesn't believe me either.

I spin around, weaving in and out of the tables through the restaurant, and make a beeline for the restroom. I'm thankful to find a private stall, and after I slam the door shut behind me, my fingers fumble as I quickly press play.

Canon is dressed in his gear, his hair disheveled like he just finished his race. One of the media crew members approaches him outside his trailer. It's short, but I catch a glimpse of him with his arms wrapped around a girl, her long strawberry-blond hair curled, and she's dressed in an orange tank top and shorts.

The woman's eyes flash over to the camera, then she quickly wipes her hand over her mouth and ducks her head, taking off out of view.

My heart leaps, zeroing in on how her hands gripped his face as if they were about to kiss.

Hitting pause, I attempt to swallow the bile rising in my throat. I squeeze my eyes shut, tears hitting me in a rush, silently praying this is all a sick joke.

It feels like the walls of the bathroom stall are starting to close in on me, and I desperately need space. I want to get out of here and back to my room, away from everyone else.

"Kyla, are you in here?" Ivy's muffled voice asks from the other side of the door.

I drag my hand over my face, wiping away the tears, and flip the lock.

"I'm sorry," I say, forcing a smile, more for myself than anything.

My mind is racing a million miles a minute. I need to call Canon and demand to know what's going on, to make sense of what I'm seeing, so he can put my mind at ease like he always does.

I walk past Ivy to the sink, shoving my phone in my pocket. She stares at my reflection in the mirror, and I do my best to remain unaffected.

"Something's wrong. What happened? Who messaged you?"

I adjust the temperature of the faucet, letting the cold water wash over my clammy fingers. I bend down and splash some over my face, not caring in the least about messing up my makeup.

I can't shake the feeling that whatever came from my conversation with Canon was about to change everything between us.

"Is it Canon?" Ivy presses, watching me as I dry my hands, then follows me out into the lobby.

The guys must've taken care of the bill because they're all standing near the door waiting for us.

"It's nothing. The food was delicious. I'm just not feeling well. It must've been from the chicken parmesan," I lie. "I think I'm gonna head back to my room and lie down."

I clutch my phone against my chest as if it's a shield protecting my heart from shattering. Questions swirl through my mind like a storm cloud as I push past Madden toward the bay of elevators.

"Go have fun. Behave. I'll see you in the morning." I wave Madden and Ivy off.

Worry and concern mar their features, but I don't have the answers to give them right now. I desperately need them for myself too.

As soon as the elevator door closes, I'm alone once again. I sag against the wall, take a deep breath, and press play on the video.

I lose track of how many times I watch the clip, pausing and scrolling back to the beginning. Each time, I analyze a different point, picking apart his smile or the closeness between them and the way she holds his face.

There's a familiarity between them until they break apart, the reporter asking for a moment of his time to ask Canon a few questions.

Canon's eyes widen, a look of guilt passing over his face when he notices the camera pointing at him. He quickly snaps out of it, putting on the same smile I've seen him wear for all his interviews. He nods, clears his throat, and turns his attention to the reporter.

I swipe my screen, going back to the text message.

Who sent this to me? How did they get my number?

I quickly type out a message, and my thumb hovers over the send button before I finally give in.

Me: Who is this?

Almost immediately, a message comes through.

Unknown: I'm not someone you should be worrying about. I just thought you deserved to know.

Somehow, the response fills me with more dread than reassurance. It's as if every worst-case scenario and fear racing through my mind is confirmed. What if there's more to this than I know?

The elevator dings and I glance up, coming face-to-face with Tysin.

His face drops, and his steps falter when he sees me standing there.

"Are you okay?" he asks.

I scrub a hand over my face, hurrying to brush the tear threatening to fall from my eye, and paste on a forced smile.

"Yeah." I sigh. "I'm just tired."

"Madden said you had an upset stomach?"

Shit. "Yeah, that too. I think I just need a good night's rest."

He nods slowly, clearly not believing me.

Tysin skips taking the elevator and walks with me down the hall to my room. I motion to mine, stopping outside the door, and pull my key card out of my pocket.

He glances down the hall before turning his gaze back to me, noticing me looking at him confused.

We haven't spoken to each other much over the past few weeks. The fact he seems to care enough to ask if I'm okay and walk me to my room is out of character.

"Have a good night," I say, flashing him another weak smile as I push my door open.

He nods but then reaches his hand out to grab my arm and stop me. I spin around quickly, and the move throws me off balance. I press my palm to his chest, trying to avoid falling against him.

He mumbles a quiet, "Sorry," under his breath. My stomach flips, and a jolt of electricity shoots through my body at our closeness.

"Do you feel it too?" he whispers.

I tilt my head back, locking my eyes on his, and my breath hitches.

"Wha-What?" I mutter.

"You and Canon."

I step back from him, breaking eye contact, unable to look at him right now.

"When you see him, does your body react the same way it does with me? Does your breath falter, and the world fall away? Is it like nothing else exists but the two of you?"

I don't know what he's doing or where he's going with this. I'm convinced this is another one of his mind games, and I can't do this with him right now.

I steel my spine, finding my resolve. "I love him," I say matter-of-factly.

"I didn't ask you if you love him, Kyla." His nostrils flare. "I'm asking you if he makes you feel alive."

Something about the softness in his eyes and the vulnerability in his words feels like he's reaching into my chest and grabbing my heart in his hand.

"Yes." I tuck a strand of hair behind my ear and nod. "He's the best thing to ever happen to me. What I feel with him, how I feel about him, is more real and intense than anything I've ever felt before."

Tysin glances down the hallway, appearing lost in thought, before he turns his eyes back to meet mine. He takes a step closer, and my mouth falls open, fumbling over my words.

I move to take a step back but find myself with my back pressed against the doorframe.

"Tysin," I whimper. "You should go."

"If you really believe those words, Kyla, then I will."

"I do."

He reaches his hand up. Only this time, he brushes his thumb beneath my eye and tilts my chin to look at him.

"If that's true, then why are you crying?"

CHAPTER TEN

KYLA

"You should go," I stammer, sidestepping into my room.

He holds his hand out, reaching for mine, and I yank my hand away from him.

"Tysin, please. Ivy and the guys are waiting for you downstairs. You need to go."

He nods once, stepping back, clenching his jaw. There's so much more he wants to say, but I shake my head, lifting my hand to wave goodbye and close the door between us.

I pull my pajamas on and walk into the bathroom to wash my makeup off when I glance in the mirror. With my bloodshot eyes and the dried mascara streaks on my face, it's no wonder I couldn't play off that I was okay.

The conversation with Tysin adds to the thoughts and questions tormenting me all night. Though I feel the urge to call

Canon, I decide against it and wait for him to call me instead. He is on the road to Michigan for a race this weekend, so he won't be checking into his hotel until late.

Except his phone call never comes.

I toss and turn all night, struggling to fall asleep. It's not until after three when I doze off, making the nine o'clock wake-up call painful, to say the least.

As much as I dread the busy day ahead, I welcome it, desperately needing anything to take my mind off the message from the night before.

The guys are amped up for their show tonight. After the short break, they're raring to go, especially since this is one of their biggest venues to date.

When you see them play, the energy fueled by the crowd is electric. I stand with Ivy, watching them from the side of the stage. I thought I caught Tysin looking in our direction a few times, but I've gotten good at convincing myself of things lately, so I tell myself it's all in my head.

Tysin's always blown me away with his skills on the guitar, and as much as he fights with Trey, they complement each other well. I'm mesmerized watching his fingers skate across the strings as he nods his head to the beat of the music.

When they finish their last song, the lights go out, and the crowd erupts, chanting for an encore. I stare out over the packed crowd, lights on their phones swaying, twinkling like stars in the sky.

They give them what they want, playing one of their earlier fan favorites, "Kiss Me Crazy." The song brings back memories of the nights I spent at Whiskey Barrel, watching them play, back to the summer I spent with Tysin.

When they storm off stage, Tysin walks right past me without a word. Sweat drips down his face, and he lifts the hem of his shirt, wiping the perspiration from his brow. He takes off down the stairs, I assume heading back toward his dressing room to shower.

"Man, that crowd was fuckin' killer tonight. I'm beat and ready for a beer," Brix groans, sauntering toward Ivy. He pulls her into his arms, and she playfully swats him on the chest.

She scrunches her nose, pulling her hand back. "You're sweaty."

"Let me get a shower, babe, and a beer in me. Then I want you back at our hotel and in my bed." He wags his brows suggestively.

Thank God I don't have to listen to them through our paper-thin walls on the bus.

"Go find somewhere else to eye-fuck each other," I scoff, muttering over my shoulder, jogging down the stairs.

Brix shouts from behind me, "You're just jealous." He follows that up by saying, "I'll let you have Ivy for the night if I can watch."

I raise my middle finger in the air and head toward the dressing rooms.

Tysin's door is open, and I poke my head inside. His shirt is off, his back facing me. I eye his Briggs tattoo spanning his upper back.

He doesn't notice me at first as he rummages through his suitcase on the counter. His eyes land on our reflection in the mirror when he glances up.

"Good show." I smile warmly.

It's a peace offering. Up until last night, every time we've spoken to each other, it's been fueled with anger. Something shifted between us, though. There's an openness I haven't seen since the night I told him I loved him two years ago.

"Thanks."

His face is blank, and my body warms from the heat of his stare. I fidget with my hands, thinking maybe I'm wrong.

"You feelin' better after last night?"

His expression softens, and I nod.

"You want to talk about it, or are you still dealing with that stomachache?"

I exhale a chuckle. He knows I was full of shit, and he's calling me on it.

"Is it Canon? He do somethin' to hurt you?"

I raise my brow. "What would make you think he hurt me?"

He turns around and leans against the edge of the counter, crossing his arms in front of his chest. His throat bobs when he swallows, but I want him to continue.

"I've seen the look on your face. The pain. Those tears weren't from you missin' him."

I sigh, walking into the room, and close the door behind me.

I want to beg him to put his shirt on. Lord knows I can't think straight with his body on display, but it doesn't matter. I need to keep this quick anyway.

"I got a text from a random number with a link to an interview he did last week. There's a video clip, and right as he was approached by the reporter, the camera, uh—it caught him in a compromising position."

His brows shoot up. "You're kidding."

I shake my head because the ache in my chest is back. I've managed to ignore it all day by numbing it with work, but standing here, talking about it for the first time, brings it all back to the surface.

It's a fresh wound, still sensitive and tender to the touch.

"What's he say about it?"

"I haven't asked him yet."

"Why?"

"I don't know." I shrug. "I guess I'm trying to convince myself it's all a misunderstanding."

Tysin pushes off the counter, crossing the space until only a foot separates us.

"Maybe it's not how it looks." He crosses his arms. "People will twist anything when you're in the public eye and make it out to be worse than it truly is. Don't you think you owe it to him to let him explain first?"

I shake my head, staring down at the floor.

"Since when did you become Dr. Phil?"

He barks out a laugh. The sound was like balm to my tattered heart. I miss this, being around him and not having the animosity and resentment between us.

"I guess I'm trying to give you an objective opinion. What does Ivy think you should do?"

I pick at my chipped fingernails. I painted them two nights ago, but I've started picking at them with all the anxiety eating away at me.

"I haven't told her yet. I wasn't even expecting to tell you."

He smirks, only this time it isn't in a devilish smile. It's full of warmth and understanding. My heart flips, knowing how dangerous it is for me to open myself up to him again.

I'm confused about what happened last night between us, and now being here, seeing this side of him is adding more conflicting thoughts swirling through my head.

"You deserve far more than you have settled for, Kyla."

"Oh, like who? You?" I roll my eyes.

He chuckles, shaking his head. "Nah, I knew you deserved better than my sorry ass a long time ago."

My face falls, and my heart seizes. "Do you really believe that?"

He lets out a self-deprecating laugh and drops his arms to his sides. "Yeah, yeah, I do."

"Why? What makes you think like that?"

"Kyla, the life you want, it's not for me. Marriage, kids—I would've never been able to give you the future you want."

I swallow hard at the mention of kids. If he only knew the truth. I couldn't bear the pain of breaking it to him two years ago, and I certainly can't do it now.

"We're cut from two different cloths. I can't even manage a relationship without fuckin' it all up. Lord knows I have no business being any child's father."

The conviction in his voice means he truly believes what he's saying. My heart sinks at the thought of him living life alone, using alcohol and meaningless relationships to fill the sting of his loneliness.

"Don't look so sorry for me," he jokes.

It's hard not to, though.

I don't know why I ask—maybe it's because he's being so raw and open right now—but the words are out of my mouth before I take the chance to reconsider them.

"You never felt anything for me, did you? It was never worth fighting past your fears and trying?"

He reaches his hand out toward me before jolting it away. As much as I wish I could take those words back, I want to know the answer.

I've spent so much time wondering why.

It feels wrong of me to ask because despite whatever feelings I have toward Canon for what I saw in the video, I'm betraying him now.

I'm no better than him.

It doesn't change the fact that I still desperately want to know the truth, even if only for my own closure. After all this time, maybe it will help me fully close the chapter of Tysin and move on.

"I was never good enough for you, Kyla. I knew it before we ever began. But like the selfish bastard I am, I saw what you were offering me, and I took it, even knowing I would break your heart in the end."

I press my palm to my chest, biting my lip to hold back my sob.

"You deserve better. Letting you go was the only way I could love you."

CHAPTER ELEVEN

KYLA

"Did you see Canon won his race?" Ivy asks. Taking a seat next to me, she tucks her legs beneath her.

We both knew how big his race in Minnesota was for him. The points he earned from this race would push him into second place in point standing.

I nod. "It's an important race. It's why I've held off on talking to him. I guess I'm also hoping he'll say or do something to make me realize it was all bullshit anyway."

Ivy pops the top of the container of Ben and Jerry's ice cream, lifting her hand to reveal two spoons. She clinks them together before handing me one.

When we got back to the hotel in Chicago, Ivy stopped by her room to check on me. She could sense something was bothering me and wanted to give me time to come forward and tell her on my own.

When I didn't, she decided it was time to pry it out of me, knowing eventually it would eat me alive. I'm thankful for it because I would've done the same if the roles were reversed.

I lean my head against my forearm, letting the sunlight and warm breeze hit my face, taking a spoonful of cookies and cream.

She lifts her spoon to cheers, and I giggle.

"To the only men who will never let us down." She laughs.

"Well, besides Jack and Jamison," I add, shoving the heaping bite into my mouth.

I moan, rolling my eyes closed.

"Have you talked to him yet?"

I shake my head, peering out the window. I'm back to avoiding things.

Avoiding Canon, avoiding Tysin, and now this conversation too.

"If I've learned anything from being with Brix, it's that some people will stop at nothing to bring others down."

It's true. I've heard stories about jealous fans and groupies who will concoct the most outrageous stories, trying to drive a wedge between her and Brix. One chick went as far as to post old photos with Brix on social media from before they were together.

"I'm betting it's not what it looks like, Kyla. Maybe it's old footage. Who knows?"

I've considered it myself, but it's not possible. The trailer in the background is the new one they bought before the season started.

"Have you heard from that number again?"

I shake my head, scraping another chunk of ice cream onto my spoon and shoveling it into my mouth. Pulling my phone out of my pocket, I scroll through my messages and click on the one from the unknown number before handing it over to Ivy.

She flips her spoon upside down, holding it in her mouth, reading over the message before the sound of the video plays.

I've watched it so many times that I know it backward and forward.

It's obvious he knows the girl. Their hug is more intimate than one you'd share with a friend. I can tell from their body language—how he has his arms around her waist and she's holding his face.

Every time I think about it, my heart aches a little more.

"I don't know." She sighs, handing me back the phone. "The thing I don't get is why would this person go out of their way to message you? What's in it for them to come between you?"

She has a point.

"Try calling them and see if they answer."

I've debated it a hundred times, wanting to know who the person is. I let my thumb hover before saying, "Fuck it," and press call.

The line rings once, and I hit the speaker button, letting Ivy listen in.

I glance over my shoulder at Madden and Brix, sitting at the dining table, playing a game of cards. They're too busy laughing and carrying on to pay attention to us. Tysin and Trey are asleep in their bunks.

The second ring starts before the line immediately clicks over to an automated message saying the number is no longer in service. I hit end and drop the phone on the cushion between us.

She scoffs, shaking her head.

"For all you know, this person set him up and messaged you trying to get under your skin to break you apart. You could be playing right into their hands. The race is over now. You have a few days until his next one. I think you two need to talk."

She's right. I can't avoid this forever.

Honestly, I'm missing him like crazy too.

He sent me a message before he fell asleep last night. We've both been busy, and he's never once made me feel bad when I couldn't respond right away.

Somehow, that fact made me feel even worse about avoiding him when he has shown me nothing but love and support.

I hate how I let my past insecurities get between us, making it harder for me to trust him.

The bathroom door slamming shut sends my head whipping around to see who was here. A sharp pain shoots up my neck.

"Who the hell was that?" I wince, turning back to Ivy.

She rolls her eyes. "Tysin."

We both reach into the container of ice cream, scooping another spoonful and lifting it to our mouths. I should probably stop now before I end up with an upset stomach.

The door flies open again, springing shut behind him. Tysin stalks across the kitchen and opens the fridge, swiping a bottle of water.

He's dressed in a pair of gym shorts with no T-shirt. My eyes trace over his sculpted chest to the tattoo spanning the length of his arm with A Rebels Havoc in big, bold letters, shaded in various grays and black.

He tilts his head back, taking a large drink, his eyes fixated on mine.

I flip the spoon in my mouth, slowly dragging it across my lips. Tysin's throat bobs, lowering the bottle to screw on the cap. He squeezes the lid, causing the veins in his forearms to pop out.

"I should go," I say to Ivy under my breath. "I need to call Canon."

Tysin clenches his jaw, finally breaking eye contact.

Ivy tells me she'll put the ice cream in the freezer in case I need it later tonight. I nod, shouldering past Tysin to rinse off my spoon.

He must've heard our conversation about Canon. The look on his face is emotionless, but I wish so badly I knew what was on his mind.

You deserve far more than you have settled for.

I crawl onto my bunk and pull the curtain shut behind me, turning on the small light near my feet. I fumble with my phone, pressing the call button next to his name. I swallow hard, listening to it ring, and exhale when he answers.

"Hello?" The words are muffled, making it hard to hear him.

"Hey," I say, trying to sound more chipper than I feel.

"What's up?" he replies flatly. There's an edginess to his tone, and I immediately regret bothering him.

"Is it a bad time?" I ask feebly.

He sighs. "No. I just have a lot going on. I'm having issues with the throttle on my bike, and it's stressing me out. I need to figure it out before our race next weekend."

"Okay," I reply curtly. "I guess you can call me when you want to talk, then."

"What's that supposed to mean?"

"Why are you being so defensive?" I question.

"Defensive? I told you I was stressed. I'm frustrated, okay? Why are you taking it personally?"

"Taking it personally?" I snicker. "Well, maybe because I haven't talked to you in a few days besides a couple of short messages. Maybe because I'm wondering what the hell is going on between us? Or maybe it's because I'm starting to wonder if you'd rather be with someone else." I huff.

"Someone else? What are you talking about?"

This time, I don't hold back. I burst out laughing, only it's not a genuine belly laugh. It's one of those cynical "you've gotta be fuckin' with me" laughs.

"Were you planning on telling me about your article with Wired Buzz, or were you gonna let me find out for myself?"

He pauses. The line goes completely silent. I hold the phone up to make sure the call is still connected before pressing it against my ear again.

I want to reach through the phone and shake him.

"Who was the girl you were with, Canon?"

"I don't know what you think you saw, but I can assure you it's not what you're insinuating."

"If it's not how it looks, why don't you explain it to me then?"

"Can we talk about this when I call you tonight?"

I exhale a chuckle. I knew things were tense before, but I hadn't realized things were this strained until now. We've grown more distant with each passing day.

I never thought it would come to this.

Tears well up in my eyes, and I do my best to blink past them. I thought about how this conversation might go ever since I got the message, but I never expected Canon to push me away when I confronted him, wanting to know the truth.

You deserve far more than you have settled for.

Tysin's words replay in my mind.

He didn't have any room to criticize Canon when he hurt me too, even if he's right.

Somewhere along the way, I started to accept far less than I deserved.

"Don't even worry about it, Canon. If you want to go out on the road and act single, you can be single. How about that?"

"What the hell is that supposed to mean?" he fires off.

"It means maybe this ring shouldn't be on my finger right now. Maybe it doesn't mean to you what you said it did when you gave it to me and asked me to marry you."

"Don't say that, Kyla!"

For the first time during this call, he's showing emotion, making me think maybe he does care. Why did it take pushing him to this point for him to show it?

"Not once did you think to tell me about the article? Did you ever consider how I'd feel when I saw it? Maybe we need to take the next few weeks apart to think about things, and at the end of the summer, we can decide if this is still what we want."

My heart is lodged in my throat when I hit "End Call" and drop the phone on my chest.

The gravity of it hits me like a ten-ton boulder.

CHAPTER TWELVE

TYSIN

Kyla's back to avoiding me again, which I can only assume means she made up with Canon.

We're on the road, heading toward New York for our next show. We decide to pull off and make a stop in a small town outside of Cleveland.

My insomnia has been torturing me since the tour began, and I was desperate for a good night's sleep. The short stay gave us a chance to get caught up on laundry and stock up on groceries too.

Everyone is tired when we board the bus the following morning. I opt to hang out in front and shoot the shit with Hank. I tell him how the band got together, and he reminisces about life on the road with the previous bands he's toured with.

We've spent most of our downtime out on the road writing new music for our upcoming album.

Music has always been an escape for me. I learned from an early age to stay in my room, keep the doors locked, and not draw any attention.

Most of the people my mom hung around with were criminals. The way their eyes would look at me, the sneer on their faces, made my skin crawl.

Those were the nights I couldn't sleep out of fear of someone breaking into my room. The loud music mixed with their shouting made it damn near impossible. I'd try to sneak out and stay with Madden or Brix if I could.

My guitar became my solace. My haven.

It gave me a way to drown out the world around me. With my guitar in my hands, I can push every other thought from my mind and focus on the strings beneath my fingers.

Some nights, I'd play my guitar until my fingers were raw and bloodied. It was my addiction. I couldn't deal with the wounds I carried with me on the inside, so I used the pain to distract me from the ones I could.

I'd wear the scars like a badge of honor.

The crew drove ahead and were already at the venue setting up when we rolled into New York City. I was eager to play, so I took off toward the stage for sound check.

"You don't think she'll bolt on us, do you?" Brix asks, leaning against the wall. I hand my guitar to Calvin, ready to head back toward my dressing room to change. "You think she'll back out of finishing the tour?"

"I have no idea." Ivy sighs. I can't see her face, but judging by her voice, she's conflicted over her friend.

"What if Canon asks her to quit and come home? I mean, of course she'll want to leave if it means fixing shit with him."

"Of course, she will. He's her fiancé, but I know the decision would weigh heavily on her. She wouldn't want to let you guys down. Especially Madden."

Brix nods, running his hand over his jaw.

The thought of Kyla leaving early has heat spreading over my body, and a wave of apprehension sweeps through me.

Brix hears me coming, turning his head toward me as I jog down the steps. A flash of concern shrouds his face, but he shakes it off quickly.

"What's up?" he asks, pushing off the wall.

His eyes flicker over to Ivy, trying to warn her not to say anything further. It's as if he thinks the thought of Kyla leaving would bother me.

I clench my jaw and shake my head.

"Nothin', I'm starving. Gonna go see what grub we have." I grunt, stalking past him.

He nods, his eyes cutting over to Ivy. I don't see Kyla anywhere.

"Have you seen a short brunette? She's probably running around in a pair of heels and carrying a clipboard?" I ask two security guards standing near the back door.

One of them tilts his head outside. "I saw her out this way."

I nod and wave, stepping past them and pushing through the door in search of Kyla.

It dawns on me I should've made sure I wouldn't end up locked out here, but before I think about it enough to care, it's too late.

The temperatures in New York are warm for August, but nothing like we're used to back home in Carolina Beach. The sun is starting to set, painting the sky a mixture of pinks, purples, and blues.

As soon as I round the corner, I see her standing near the front of the bus. Her damn clipboard is pressed against her chest with her phone to her ear as she paces back and forth.

She's wearing different clothes than I saw her in earlier, dressed in jeans with the front torn to shit and a black Rolling Stones T-shirt. The material is tied at the waist, showing a hint of tan skin underneath, and her long brown hair is pulled up and away from her face.

My eyes trail over her slender frame, taking the opportunity to drink her in when no one is around. I hate letting myself think about her for too long. The memories of how I hurt her still tear me up when I do.

She's so damn beautiful, though, like a fuckin' angel.

She was my angel, too, all those years ago. She never knew it, and I'd never tell a soul, but she was there for me in ways she'll never understand.

Kyla was always a light sleeper, whereas Madden could have a freight train barreling down the tracks next to him, and he wouldn't even flinch.

There were nights when my mom would invite men over, the ones that left me feeling uneasy. Those were the nights I made a break for it, climbing out of my bedroom window and taking off running down the alley.

The sound of rocks crunching now reminds me of my feet pounding against the pavement all the way to their house.

On the nights when I knew Madden was asleep, I threw rocks at Kyla's window.

She was always there, ready to let me in. No questions asked.

Some nights, I wondered if she lay awake waiting for me.

There's no way in hell Madden would've let me date his sister back then. Not only was she younger than us, but Madden also knew, as much as I did, that I wasn't good enough for her.

It didn't stop me from wishing I was, though.

When I showed up at Breaking Waves to talk to her boss, Garrett, about some work I needed to have done on my motorcycle and saw her, it was like the dam broke. I couldn't hold myself back anymore. I saw it in her eyes and felt the tension in the air. When she walked out the door after her shift to find me waiting for her, her beaming smile said it all.

The closer I get to her standing outside our bus, the more it feels like it did that day.

I watch as she hangs up the phone and slides it back into her pocket, turning back to face me. Her body freezes, her eyes holding mine.

"Hey," she says when I reach her. Her arms drop to her side.

"You forgave him?"

Her brow furrows, and she tilts her head to the side. "'Scuse me?"

"Pretty Boy," I quip. "You forgave him?"

Her hand turns into a fist, popping it against her hip. "What does it matter to you?"

She raises her brow. I curl the edge of my lip at the sight of her throwing her sass back at me.

God, she loves getting under my skin.

"Tell me, Tysin. Why do you keep asking questions about my relationship with Canon? Hell, you made it clear how you felt having me on tour with you. We made a deal to stay out of each other's way. I've done everything I can to stand by my word, yet you somehow keep finding your way back into my business."

I grit my teeth because she has a point. As hard as I try, I can't seem to keep myself away from her.

"I guess I didn't expect you to let him walk all over you too."

Her mouth drops open, her face turning red from the anger simmering under the surface. She takes a few steps toward me, closing the distance until we're standing toe-to-toe.

She tilts her head back to stare up at me. My gaze takes in the subtle rise and fall of her chest.

"Why do you want to go out of your way to prove how much of an asshole you can be to me? It's like you get off on hurting me."

"I'm only asking before you cut out of here and run back to him, leaving us high and dry."

She fumbles over her words, not expecting me to call her out on it.

"I'm here to do a job," she replies flatly. "What happens in my relationship is none of your concern and plays no role in what I'm here to do. I'm not going anywhere. Guess that means you have four more weeks to continue getting on every one of my last fuckin' nerves."

I smirk, and she rolls her eyes, shaking her head.

"You want to make me hate you, don't you?"

My smile falters, and my gaze narrows on hers. "I thought you already did."

Her throat bobs when she swallows. Her eyes glance past me, considering her answer, before meeting mine again.

"If you would've asked me before the tour began, I would've convinced myself I do. The real, honest answer is no. I don't hate you. I know you want me to, though. You think if I hate you, it'll be easier to be around me. I could never hate you, even if you deserve it, because how I feel about you could never compare to how you feel about yourself."

Ouch.

I force a swallow and press my lips together, running my hand over my jaw.

"I hope you forgave Canon, Kyla."

She rolls her eyes and shakes her head, crossing her arms over her chest.

"It's clearly what you want, but take it from me, it's only a matter of time before he hurts you again."

"Since you keep bringing it up, I didn't forgive him. I ended our engagement."

My face falls, and I wish I could take it back.

"Kyla ..." I reach out for her, but she pulls back.

"I told him to take the summer to figure out what he wants. So, to answer your question, I won't be leaving to run back home to him, and no, I haven't forgiven him. Is that what you want to hear? Are we done now?"

"Look, I'm sorry. I shouldn't have said anything."

"Fuck off, Tysin," she fires off.

She lowers her shoulder, catching me in the arm when she stalks past me.

I fight the urge to reach out and grab her hand to stop her. To lift her over my shoulder and carry her onto the bus, where no one else can see us.

The same way I did the last night we were together.

I'll never forgive myself for how I hurt her, letting her walk into my house to find two girls on top of me.

I was still reeling from my fight with Brix over our bet and how it put him in hot water with Ivy.

All I wanted to do was drink until I could forget my fuckin' name.

I didn't expect to look up and find her standing there watching me. The pain and torment in her eyes have eaten away at me since that night.

I should've let her leave right then and there, but I didn't.

I couldn't.

Neither one of us wanted to talk, and I used her pain to cover up my own.

I hate you.

I tore down her pants and fucked her against the wall until our bodies shuddered with the force of our release. My fingers gripped her hair, my teeth marking her skin, and she loved every second of it.

I hate you.

In the heat of the moment, we forgot where we were and what we were doing.

I love you.

Those three words were on the tip of my tongue when I came inside her. I wanted so badly to return those feelings, but I couldn't.

I couldn't bring myself to hurt her any more than I already had. I would never be good enough for her, and that night was proof of it.

I hate you.

Those were the last words she said to me, and until today, I was convinced she meant them.

I guess we've both been lying to ourselves.

CHAPTER THIRTEEN

KYLA

We're back on the road, off to our next tour stop.

Maybe it's the exhaustion or the days blurring together, but I can't remember where we're heading next.

I put my earbuds in, and am about to turn over, when I hear a rustling sound come from Tysin's bunk above me. I pause my music, holding my breath, attempting to figure out the sound.

My body freezes when I hear Tysin's muffled groans mix with the thrashing of his body.

"Tysin."

My words come out raspy, my heart hammering in my chest as I scramble to pull my curtain back and push myself to stand.

"No, no, no ..." he mutters.

I quickly fling his curtain back, tossing my phone and earbuds on my mattress. His bunk comes up to my chest, making it hard to see him.

I step onto my bed, hoisting myself up, and climb next to him.

His skin is hot with beads of sweat dripping from his forehead. His body trembles, his head whipping from side to side. I reach over and grip his shoulder, trying to wake him.

He squeezes his eyes tighter, almost as if he's wincing in pain.

"Tysin." I shake him again.

Each time I do, I pull back, afraid I'll catch him off guard.

It's futile, though. His body shudders. The words he once spoke with venom are now mixed with defeat.

"No, no, no." The desperation in his voice makes my heart ache.

I don't know what to do to help him.

I pull his blankets back and curl up next to him, wrapping my arms around his body, draping my legs over him to do the same.

For a second, I worry it isn't going to work. Tremors wrack his body, his skin slick with sweat under my hands as I hold him.

When he mutters, "Why," spoken with so much pain, I don't bother holding back the tears filling my eyes.

I wish he'd wake up.

I softly whisper to him, reassuring him everything will be okay, pressing my palm to the side of his face.

"Tysin, please wake up. Please come back to me," I whisper, tucking my head against his shoulder.

His body goes lax, and he sucks in a deep breath, frantically looking around him.

"It's okay," I whisper. "It's just me."

It's dark in his bunk, only a sliver of light peeking through from the hallway.

For a second, I wonder if he realizes who I am before his soft voice murmurs, "Kyla?"

"Yeah ..."

"You're here? What are you doing in my bunk?"

"You were having a bad dream. I didn't know what to do. I tried to wake you up, but when that didn't work ..."

"You mean I'm not dreaming?"

The pain is back in his voice. The thought of him thinking me here with him, alone in his bed, was all a dream, made my heart seize.

"You're awake. I'm here."

He exhales, his hand reaching over his body to grip mine, and he mumbles, "You're here."

A million questions flood my head, but I don't dare voice them out loud.

He relaxes, and I don't bother moving, keeping my legs and arms wrapped around him like vines weaving their way up a trellis.

I know me staying here, holding him like this, is crossing a line. I can imagine how hurt I'd be if Canon did the same.

The thought of Canon has me pulling my arm back before Tysin wraps his hand around my wrist, stopping me.

"I'm sorry," he murmurs.

For a second, I think he's talking about our fight outside the bus. I consider asking him why the thought of me forgiving Canon bothers him so much.

Whatever he was dreaming was clearly bothering him, so I file it away for another time.

"Do you want to talk about it? Your dream?"

"No."

The word is harsh, straight to the point, and without an ounce of second-guessing.

"Maybe someday ..." he adds, his tone softening. "Not right now, though. I don't want to burden you with my bullshit tonight."

I want to say something to refute his comment, reassuring him there's nothing he could say that would ever be a burden.

"You know you can trust me, right?"

We lie there for a moment, his hand holding mine, leaving my question hanging in the air.

He drags his thumb over my skin. For a second, I almost wonder if I'm dreaming myself.

"I do," he whispers.

A part of me believes Tysin wants to open up, and his reassurance of maybe someday he will, feel as if there's more I could miss out on if I pull back now.

"Are you feeling better?"

"Yeah." He turns his head to look down at me. "Thank you again."

My eyes meet his in the dimly lit space, and I nod, resting my chin on his shoulder.

"Will you do me a favor, though?" he asks.

"Of course. What is it?"

He turns his head back toward the ceiling and exhales. I stare at his face, waiting for him to respond. I swear, a small smile plays on his lips, and he chuckles under his breath.

"You shouldn't have agreed before you knew what the favor was."

"Spill it, Briggs," I jest.

He squeezes my hand. "Stay here with me."

All playfulness we shared a moment ago is gone once the words pass his lips.

"Listen, I know what I'm asking you, and I'm sorry. I just … I don't want to be alone tonight. Stay with me. Let me hold you."

"Tysin."

"Kyla—"

"I don't think it's a good idea," I lie.

"Please."

The ache in his voice sounds like the same pain I heard when I first climbed in his bunk with him.

Truth be told, I want so badly to forget the world outside this bus and stay here with him, to pretend nothing else exists and the past never happened.

I start to think about how hard this will be tomorrow when the lights turn on and we go back to real life.

I wish things had been different between us that summer.

Tysin is no stranger to one-night stands and no strings attached. I didn't want to be another distraction, a way for him to cover up whatever he's dealing with.

I couldn't blame him, though. It's easy for me to forget about Canon, and where things stand with us, being here with him too.

I exhale a heavy breath, shoving my hand under his pillow.

Tysin turns his body to face me, my arms and legs wrapped around him. I debate pulling back and giving him space until his hand skates over my hip and pulls me closer to him.

He stretches his arm under his pillow, too, his hand finding mine, lacing our fingers together. He rubs his thumb over the back of my hand again, and my breath hitches, making it hard to breathe.

There's no denying the calmness that sweeps over us, the quiet stillness around us. Minutes later, I hear his breathing even out as sleep pulls him under.

My eyes adjust to the darkness and take in his long lashes spread across his cheekbones. There's a peacefulness to him that wasn't there before.

I wish I knew what made him believe with so much passion and reverence it was better for him to stay away from me or what made him want me here with him now.

"What are we doing, Tysin?" I murmur between us.

His arm around my waist tightens, and I tuck my head under his chin, letting him hold me.

It's as if he knows I'm here with him, and he releases a soft sigh.

I remember the nights when I would've given anything to be here with him. I squeeze my eyes shut, soaking in the feel of his body against mine, letting out a sigh of my own.

When sleep pulls me under, it's one of the best nights of rest I've had in months.

CHAPTER FOURTEEN

TYSIN

"You sure you don't want to come with us?" Ivy asks, reaching her hand out for Kyla's.

Hank pulls in, parking the bus near the back of Twisted Whiskey.

Trey's been itching to hit up a club since we got on the road, and it took no convincing to get everyone else on board.

Ivy chews on her lip, looking back and forth between Kyla and Brix.

"Yeah." She smiles, reassuring Ivy. "I could use some time to myself anyway."

Knowing Kyla is hanging back here alone has me thinking through ways I could pull out somehow and stay here with her without raising any eyebrows.

Ivy is still worried about Kyla and how she's handling things with Canon. If she had any idea Kyla snuck into my bunk the other night, there's no telling the reaction we'd get.

It's safe to say she's not my biggest fan.

"What kind of quiet time?" Trey jokes, resting his boot on the couch next to her, nudging her leg playfully.

I'm ready to strangle the motherfucker the moment he does.

Thankfully, Madden is right there, doing my dirty work for me.

"Nuh-uh, fucker. Get that thought right out of your head. That's my sister, you hear me?"

Trey grins, flashing Kyla a wink. She shakes her head, cracking a smile. This one more genuine than the one she gave Ivy.

I want to beat his ass now.

"Yeah, yeah, I know." He chuckles. "I'm not about to tangle myself up in some shit."

He holds his hands up in surrender, attempting to reassure Madden. His eyes flash over to mine, and his lip curls in a smirk, knowing he's getting under my skin too.

I lift my finger behind Madden's back, flipping him off, and Trey laughs.

"I doubt I'll be out too late. If you're up for it, when I get back, we can have a late-night pamper sesh in our room," Ivy adds.

Brix groans, muttering about how he won't be getting laid tonight.

He hasn't been able to keep his hands off Ivy since she strutted out of their room wearing a pair of ankle breakers.

I plop down on the couch and stare at my hands, watching as everyone makes their way off the bus. Madden and Hank shake hands. Madden claps him on the back when Hank reassures him he'll look after things.

Everyone files off the bus, leaving the two of us alone.

Kyla is standing in the kitchen, leaning against the counter, sipping on a cup of coffee with one foot crossed in front of the other.

"You sure you'll be all right here alone?"

She nods. "You don't have to worry about me. I'll be fine."

"I'm not sure if Ivy knows what's going on with you," I say. Her face falls. "I know better than to believe a woman when she says she's fine."

We haven't spoken again about Canon or acknowledged the night she crawled into bed with me.

I don't want to press her further, but I also don't want to miss the chance to be with her again. Alone.

She exhales a laugh. "Yeah, I guess you're right. I have Hank here with me. I'll be just fine."

"Yo, Tysin. You comin' or what?" Brix hollers onto the bus.

I grit my teeth and shake my head, wishing they would've gone ahead without me.

"I doubt I'll be gone long myself. I'm not feeling it tonight, so I'm sure I'll be seein' ya soon."

She purses her lips together, and I swear it's to fight off the smile I see peeking through. She nods, back to her fake reassuring bullshit she's been feeding everyone these days.

"All right, well, I'm gonna shower and do a face mask. You won't be missing out on much," she jokes, turning to walk down the hall toward our bunks.

My eyes track her movements, down to the red cotton shorts she's wearing with the white trim along the bottom.

I've always had a thing for Kyla in red.

The club is packed to the nines, with a line wrapping around the front of the building. Abel spoke to one of the bouncers, so we are admitted without questions.

The lights are low, and it takes a second for my eyes to adjust to the darkness. The music thumps while I lean against the bar overlooking the club, nursing my lone beer. I'm letting the time tick by before I slip out of here, and I know if I don't have a beer in my hand at all times, someone will end up asking questions.

It's after midnight when I tell the guys I'm going to turn in and head back to the bus. They're too busy having fun to press me on it.

All I've been able to think about is Kyla on the bus alone and wishing I was there with her. As I'm weaving my way through the crowd of people, I get the idea to swing by the gas station across the street.

Thankfully, it's quiet by this time of night. The cashier recognizes me when I walk through the door, her wide eyes tracking me through the store. We snap a few pictures after she rings me up, and I take off back to the bus.

"I wasn't expecting you to be back so soon." Kyla laughs when I climb the steps a few minutes later.

She's seated on the couch with her hair pulled up twisted in one of those messy buns. If she hadn't warned me earlier, I'd be wondering what the hell the pink shit is smeared all over her face.

"You weren't even gone an hour," she says, snapping me out of my wayward thoughts.

"I told you I wasn't feelin' it tonight. What's this shit you're watching?"

"I have no idea, honestly. I turned the TV on when applying my lotion and got sucked into whatever was playing."

My eyes burn into her legs from where they're sprawled out across the couch. Her red toenails poke out from under the blanket covering her lap.

What I wouldn't give to explore all the ways I could make them curl in pleasure, and it causes my dick to harden.

Every inch of her body turns me on.

"Wanna watch a movie?" I ask, my voice cracking. I clear my throat, attempting to cover up the desire zipping through me.

Her eyes go wide, and she nods. I wonder if she's thinking back to the night we spent together. What started off as watching a movie led to us having sex on my couch.

It was also the night she told me she loved me.

"Yeah." She moves her legs to curl them beneath her, giving me room to sit next to her. "Another scary movie?"

Turns out she was thinking back to that night, after all.

"I came prepared too." I grin, holding the bag of sour gummy worms in the air.

Her eyes flicker, staring down at the bag, and she sucks in a breath. Memories of her teasing me, brushing the sour sugar over her lips before she kissed me, scroll through my mind like a highlight reel.

"Are you serious?" She giggles. She moves to kneel on the couch, clapping enthusiastically when I toss the bag in her direction.

"We're never gonna be able to fall asleep with all this candy." She snickers.

"Who cares? We have nothing going on tomorrow anyway. We can pull an all-nighter."

"Really? You want to?"

I nod. "There's nowhere else I want to be."

I sit next to her, and she plops down, moving the blanket over her lap. I reach for the remote and flick through the horror movies.

She shakes her head, tossing a piece of candy in her mouth.

“You and your scary movies,” she jokes.

I shrug. “If I’m lucky, maybe I’ll have you curled up next to me again.”

It was meant to be a joke, but when her face falls, I know the error of my ways.

I’m not sure if it’s the insinuation of us together or what came after that night, but I wish I could press rewind and take it back.

“Sorry, my bad. I probably shouldn’t have—”

She darts her hand out to stop me, and I stare down at where her hand grips my forearm. Almost as if she’s trying to stop me from saying anything more.

“I’m sorry.” She pulls her hand back as if touching me seared her skin. “It’s okay, really. I’d love to hang out and watch a movie. I could use the distraction right now.”

“All right.” I swallow hard.

My arm tingles from where she touched me. I wish I knew what she was thinking right now.

“I’m gonna wash this off my face. I'll be a couple of minutes. You can start the movie.” She motions to her face and smiles.

“Actually, I think I’m gonna change real quick too.”

We both stand, and I let her go in front of me, taking the opportunity to check out her ass in those fuckin’ shorts. I’m gonna need a minute just to tame the hard-on growing in my pants at the sight of her hips swaying in front of me.

She takes the bathroom, and I slip into the back bedroom to change. I’m standing in front of the TV, scrolling through a list of movies, when her bare feet pad across the tile floor toward me.

She curls up under her blanket again, popping another piece of candy in her mouth. She's fresh-faced, highlighting the faint freckles dotting the apples of her cheeks. My fingers itch to touch her skin, remembering how silky smooth it felt against my rough fingertips.

Without breaking eye contact, I click on the newest *Halloween* movie, and the music plays.

"You remember." She stares up at me, an emotion I can't quite read passing over her face.

I nod, taking the seat next to her.

She chews on her gummy treat, her tongue darting out to swipe the sugar from her lips.

Fuck me, I wish I could lean over and have a taste.

"I remember everything."

She lifts another piece to her mouth when I say it, her hand pausing in the air before she slowly lowers it to her lap.

"You do?"

How do I tell her every memory is painfully etched into my mind?

Her sunglasses and how they matched her red lipstick. The shorts she wore over her aqua-blue swimsuit and how they practically had me salivating at the sight of her.

How the smell of coconut reminds me of the two of us standing in Breaking Waves. I want to tell her how every time I've heard Three Days Grace, I'm reminded of her singing along to the lyrics in my truck.

I wish I could tell her how much it meant to me when she said those three words. I want her to know it tore me up inside, knowing we'd never be anything more.

And how the hatred and the pain in her eyes the last night we were together have eaten away at me like poison in my blood.

"Everything." My voice breaks.

She stares wordlessly at me, something flickering in her eyes. An emotion I couldn't quite name.

I don't want to do this to her now. She's moved on and found love with Canon. The last thing I want to do is dredge up all the past pain and hurt again.

I deserve every ounce of pain and anger I've carried with me, knowing what I did to her.

Even if it makes me even more of a selfish bastard, I want to soak up every second with her for as long as I can. It's only a matter of time before the tour wraps up, and she'll go back home to Canon. They'll make up, get married, and move on with their lives.

And me? I'll be here, back on the road making music, and these memories will be all I have left of her.

I reach into her lap and grab a few gummy worms. I toss one into my mouth and playfully grin at her. The seriousness of the moment breaks, and she smiles back, turning to face the screen.

"Good ole Michael Myers." She chuckles.

We joke throughout the movie about how it always seems like the people walk right into danger without a second thought.

A few times, I find myself peering over at her, taking in her smile and the sound of her laughter. When the silence falls between us and sleep pulls her under, she unconsciously leans her head against my shoulder and curls up against my side.

There will come a time when this moment will haunt me.

For now, I'll put it out of my mind and just soak in having her next to me again.

Even if it'll torture me later.

CHAPTER FIFTEEN

KYLA

Their show in Atlanta is one of their biggest yet. It's a sold-out crowd. Even though they'll never admit it, Trey and Tysin have been playing well together.

I'm racing around like a chicken with my head cut off, trying to get everyone where they need to be. It's eased some tension between the guys by not having them bicker.

Lord knows it's saved me a headache or two as well.

By the time the guys get back to their dressing room to shower and their equipment is loaded, I'm ready to call it a night and get the hell out of here.

Madden and Brix are already on the bus, leaving me with Trey, Tysin, and Ivy. Ivy stayed with me while I wrapped everything up with the event director.

"I can't wait to get back to the hotel and have a beer," Trey grumbles, taking off toward the bus.

My body aches. I could go for a shower and a beer right about now, although I'm not certain I'll make it that far.

We have five days off before the next show. We decided to start heading north toward Indianapolis and find a few spots to stay along the way.

My phone vibrates in my pocket, and I pull it out, checking the screen to see a message come through from an unknown number.

Every time I get a call or message from a number I don't recognize, my stomach twists in knots with the anxiety about what it could be.

I've been holding out hope I'd hear from Canon tonight, so when I see this, it's as if my heart is lodged in my throat.

My footsteps falter, stopping me in my tracks. Ivy and Tysin both turn back toward me, probably noticing the halting sound of my clicking heels on the concrete.

"Who is it?" Ivy asks.

I pick up on the note of panic in her tone. I shake my head, not sure how to reply, and click on the video. It's dark around me, much like on the screen, making it easier for my eyes to adjust.

I fold my hand over my mouth, unable to resist the urge to replay it. Tears prick my eyes, and not even my hand can contain my wail.

Ivy rushes toward me, pulling the phone from my hands. Tysin and Trey are right behind her. I stare up at Trey's frantic face when Tysin wraps his arms around my waist, catching me before my weak knees send me collapsing to the ground.

"I'm gonna kill him," Ivy grits out without an ounce of emotion in her voice.

Tears stream down my face, and my body shudders. I turn to bury my head in Tysin's chest.

"What is it? What happened?" Trey asks.

He leans his head down into my shoulder, whispering into my ear that it'll be okay.

He's wrong. I want to push him away and tell him to shut up, but I can't speak. I can't even move.

Ivy wraps her arms around me, and I turn into her. Tysin reaches to grab the phone before I snatch it away from him.

I know it's Canon from his black Watt racing T-shirt and the Miami Blaze hat he's wearing from our Florida trip. His distinctive tattoo covering the length of his arm was the first thing I noticed when I opened the video, removing any doubt in my mind about whether it was him.

It's him, and the knot coiling in my stomach is evidence of it too.

A million questions race through my mind.

Who is it? Who would be worth risking it all and throwing our relationship away for?

My fingers move without thought, scanning through my phone to click on his name and connect the call.

I note the time is after three in the morning. Then briefly consider if he doesn't answer, who could he possibly be with?

It's barely a thought in my mind when his gruff voice filters through the line.

I push myself away from Ivy and Tysin.

"Canon?"

Ivy reaches for my hand, but I wave her off. I don't want her trying to stop me now. I've held this in for too long.

"Leave her alone," Tysin urges her.

Ivy's gaze darts over to him, and she curls her lip in anger.

"You don't give a shit about what this will do to her, Tysin. You're only thinking about what this means for yourself. You selfish son of a bitch."

"You don't know a goddamn thing about how I feel," he growls.

I wave my arm between them, desperate for them to shut up. A part of me wants to know what Tysin means, but my thoughts are ricocheting back and forth like a ping pong ball. I can't keep up.

Canon repeats my name in my ear, snapping me back to the reason I called.

"Tell me," I blurt out, my voice clipped. "I just had a video of you with another woman sent to me. Tell me. Who is it?"

Rustling sounds through the line. I picture him in bed, wearing his boxer briefs and his hair disheveled.

"Canon ..." I trail off.

"Can we do this face-to-face?" he pleads.

Face-to-face? How could he possibly think I want to look at him after what I saw?

"I'm not waiting."

"Let me FaceTime you," he begs. "Please."

"Just tell me. Don't drag this out. Just fuckin' spit it out already."

"It's not what it looks like."

I toss my head back and laugh. The sound comes out maniacally from deep in my throat.

"I don't give a shit what it looks like, Canon. I want to know the truth. The facts. Starting with who the fuck it is and why did it look like you were kissing her?"

Another sigh follows, and the rustling continues. I look up, finding Tysin staring back at me. His arms are crossed in front of his chest, his brow furrowed. He swallows hard and winces.

Behind him, Ivy paces back and forth, rubbing her hands together. I half expect her to rattle off a plan of how we'll seek vengeance when I hang up. I'll be right behind her, ready to load up the car, knowing she'd be down for whatever I throw her way.

"Say something." I snarl. "I want answers. Now."

I stalk away from Tysin and Ivy, needing a second to collect myself without them eavesdropping. The moment I turn the corner around the back of the bus, I burst into tears.

"Please. Please just tell me."

"I'm sorry. I didn't mean for it to happen."

"Stop. Stop apologizing, especially when you don't mean it. I deserve to know what's going on and who you were with, Canon."

"It was after a race. I went out with the guys for a few drinks, and I ran into someone. An old friend of mine."

I'm not stupid. I know about his past relationships, so when he mentions an old friend, my mind immediately goes to her.

Savannah.

Tysin is to me what Savannah is to Canon.

He never went into detail about their history, but I knew enough to know that much.

Growing up, Canon said his parents kept him on a short leash. He wasn't allowed to go out, much less have a girlfriend. They wanted all his attention kept on school and racing.

It wasn't until he went off to college that they met. Only their family histories run much deeper than that. Savannah's family is deep in the motocross world too. Her two older brothers were Canon and Cove's biggest rivals.

"It was her, wasn't it?" I mumble.

We both knew who I was talking about without mentioning her name. I know without asking that the person from the Wired Buzz article was her too.

"I need you to know I never expected this to happen."

"You never expected for it to happen or for me to find out?"

"Neither." He sighs, his voice growing panicked. "I didn't even know she was in town. It's not like I planned for this."

"Did you fuck her?"

"What? No!" he shouts. He goes silent.

I picture him pacing his bedroom, dragging his hand over his head, squeezing his eyes shut the way he does when he's frustrated.

"It was a kiss. It was only a kiss. It didn't mean anything. I swear to God."

"It must have meant something, or you would've told me about it before I found out, Canon."

The line goes silent. He knows I'm right. We talked about this, how our relationship will be tested when we're out on the road. We promised going into this that we'd always be honest with each other.

My mind filters back to the night I crawled into Tysin's bunk with him and held him. I wonder if I was in the wrong, too, for not telling Canon. In my mind, it's different. I was there for a friend, but the level of intimacy and betrayal was different.

Although, in the back of my mind, a voice shouts at me that I'm wrong.

"I don't think I can do this ..." I mutter.

"Do what? Be with me?"

"I don't know. I think we knew this would happen. We knew the temptations would be there."

"Then come home to me. Come out on the road. We'll talk about everything and work this out."

"I can't, Canon. I can't just leave the guys. I made a promise to my brother, and I won't back out on him."

"You also made a promise to me."

"Don't go there, Canon. You made the same promise when you gave me this ring." I stare down at my finger, the diamond glimmering beneath the parking lot lights.

He exhales. "You're right. It's just, it's just hard to be away from you. It's hard not being able to see you right now."

"I can't." My voice cracks.

Silence falls over us. My chest aches, feeling like it's starting to cave in as my heart breaks.

I thought we were in this together. We had our future all mapped out. How is it that a few weeks of being away from each other has caused the foundation we built and the life we laid out to begin to crumble beneath our feet?

"I need time," I admit. "I need to sort out my thoughts, what this means, and what I want."

"Does this mean we're over?"

"I don't know, Canon. Up until fifteen minutes ago, before I got that message, I would've said no. Now ... now I don't know."

"Message?"

"I got another text message," I announce. "This time, it wasn't an article. It was just a video of the two of you together. The sight of you, her legs wrapped around your waist. It's not something I can unsee. I can't just forget what you've done. I think you need time too."

"Why the fuck do I need time?" he growls. "And another? Who the hell is sending this shit to you?"

"I don't know!" My body tenses, and I stomp my foot as I grit my teeth and shout into the phone. Tears stream down my face again, the pounding in my head making me wince.

"I don't need time," he snaps, each word punctuated this time.

I laugh. "Well, I think you're wrong."

"So, what, you're gonna go out on the road and get back at me?" He chuckles. "Don't act like you don't have your own temptation there too."

"As far as I'm concerned, we're over Canon. It's done. You're free to live your life and do as you please, but it looks like you've already been doing that since our last conversation."

"Kyla, please," he begs.

"I guess it's time for me to do the same." I exhale, pressing the end button.

I lean against the bus, sliding down to the ground, and let the tears wrack my body.

Tysin appears a moment later, and Ivy isn't too far behind. He doesn't say a word when he bends down and lifts me into his arms.

Ivy chews on her lip. The look on her face says she's doing everything she can to bite her tongue, so she doesn't say whatever is on her mind.

I know better, though. It'll all come out eventually.

I tuck my head against his neck and whisper, "Thank you."

"Anything for you."

CHAPTER SIXTEEN

KYLA

I'm grateful the guys agree to go straight to Indianapolis and skip our plans to break it out over the next five days.

It takes us a couple of days, but we finally pull into town. I'm desperate for a shower and a good night's sleep.

Canon called a few times before I finally answered and begged him to give me space. When he insisted on talking, I threatened to block his number.

I'll talk to him eventually. Right now, I just need time and space.

I took this job as a favor to my brother, and I plan to hold up my end of the deal. I know from experience it's best to keep yourself busy, but I was thankful we had a break in our schedule before their next show.

My world was beginning to feel like it was crashing down around me, and I needed time to collect my thoughts.

The first two days were spent sulking in my hotel room. Ivy stayed with me one night, and we cleared out the hotel minibar. On the second day, the hangover knocked me on my ass, so I spent all day curled in bed, living off room service.

Ivy stormed into my room earlier, insisting I couldn't wallow like this forever. It was our last night in town, so I forced myself out of bed to get ready. It wasn't until I stood in the shower, beneath the hot water, that I finally let myself break down and cry again.

I take my time washing my hair, shaving, and exfoliating. I'm standing in front of the mirror with a towel around my body, combing through my hair, when two knocks rap against the door.

I don't bother looking in the peephole, expecting it to be Ivy or Madden checking in on me. When I open the door, I'm surprised to find none other than Tysin standing on the other side.

He's dressed in dark denim jeans and a black T-shirt. His hair is longer on top than normal. The other day, he was just saying he needs to find a barber in town, but damn, does he look good.

My eyes drop to the tattoo covering his arm, disappearing beneath his sleeve, showing near the neckline of his shirt.

His eyes do some looking of their own. He scans over my body, his gaze burning into my skin. It isn't until then that I remember where I am and what I'm wearing, or I guess not wearing.

I adjust my grip on my towel, holding it against me out of fear it could be singed off my body.

"What's up?" I ask, attempting to sound nonchalant.

He clears his throat, forcing his eyes to meet mine, noticing the change in my hair color.

"You decided to go back to purple, huh?"

A smile plays at his lips, and I nod.

"I guess it was time for a change."

"We're about to head out for a bit. Grab dinner and check out this arcade downtown. Wanna join us?"

I desperately need to get out of this hotel room.

"Yeah, if you guys can give me twenty minutes, I'll get ready quick."

He nods and takes a step back, his eyes quickly glancing down my body before he lifts his hand in a wave.

Sometimes I wish I knew what he was thinking, and now is one of them.

"I'm meeting them downstairs at the bar. We'll wait there for you."

"I'll make it a quickie." I grin, joking.

His face falls, his eyes boring into mine.

I giggle, taking a step back, and wag my brows. He shakes his head, not at all amused as, I let the door slam shut.

I hurry to do my hair and get ready, settling on minimal make-up. I'm confident you can dress any look up with some red lipstick.

I take the elevator to the lobby, not wanting to leave the group waiting for me. They're standing crowded around a high-top table near the bar's entrance, chatting and drinking.

The guys appear to be a beer or two in, laughing and joking animatedly. Ivy stands next to Brix in black shorts and a green top, showing off the ivy tattoo wrapped around her leg.

"You're here." She smiles.

Madden's right behind her, wrapping his arm around me in a hug. He can be a big grump sometimes, but once you get past his hard shell, he's a teddy bear.

"You good?" he murmurs against the side of my head.

I nod, looking past him. My gaze falls on Tysin and the bottle of water in his hand.

He appears to be the only one in the group not drinking.

"Let's go," Tysin urges, motioning toward the door with his head.

A black SUV waits for us outside, and we all climb in. Madden barks out an address, which is good since none of us have the slightest clue where we're going.

When we pull up outside of Token City a few minutes later, the guys jump out of the car and rush inside like they're teenagers eager to play the games.

The lights are dim, with rope lights lining the walls and ceiling in a mixture of red, purple, green, and yellow.

I haven't eaten anything all day since my stomach has been in knots. Ivy has the same thought I do and reaches for my hand, pulling me toward the concession area and forcing me to order a slice.

"How are you doing?" she asks once we have our pizza and search for a table away from the crowd.

"I promise, I'm okay. I'd tell you if I wasn't," I say.

I can see in her eyes that she's concerned, but she keeps the conversation off Canon, and I'm grateful for it. She's worried, though. We both know how deep my depression was after what happened with Tysin. Just when I started to move on from him, it was like I was grieving the loss twice.

"I know." She sighs, slipping out of the booth and pulling me in for a hug.

"If you want me to kick his ass, all you have to do is say the word."

I giggle. "I know you would, just like I'd still beat Brix's ass if you'd let me."

She laughs. We both know he's deserved it a time or two.

"I'm serious, though. If you need anything, I'm always here for you."

"I know you are. I've never once questioned that either." I nod, reassuring her. "I honestly don't want to think about it anymore. I want to forget everything for tonight and have some fun."

When I look out into the crowd, I spot Tysin standing next to Madden, who is hunched over a game. He's easy to spot through the hordes of people. Our eyes lock when he notices me looking his way.

Ivy grabs my hand when we finish our slices, urging me to come with her. We grab our plates to throw them away and weave through the crowd toward the guys.

Madden is in a heated game of *Ms. Pac-Man*. His hands tap furiously on the buttons while she zooms across the screen, eating the dots.

Trey and Brix are seated on two motorcycles beside him, leaning from side to side as they race through the city streets. Ivy takes off to watch them, cheering Brix on.

Seeing them race makes me think of Canon, but I refuse to think about him now. I want to enjoy getting out for the night, not weigh myself down more. I glance over at Tysin, and a dark look passes over his face as he stares back at me.

Dragging my teeth over my lower lip, I run my hand through my hair, trying to avoid feeding into his hungry gaze.

I give in, though, unable to resist the temptation.

"I'm gonna run to the bathroom quick," I shout over the music.

When Tysin nods, I narrow my eyes. Does he think I'm talking to him?

"Okay," Madden says absentmindedly. He's too zoned out on his game to pay any attention to me.

I trace my tongue over my lips, wetting them, and adjust my purse on my shoulder. I search for any sign of the restrooms, and Tysin nods behind me.

Before I have a chance to move, I feel his chest pressed against my side, leaning in close to my neck to whisper, "I'll join you."

I don't let myself overthink it as I take off in the direction of the sign. His presence looms behind me until I escape into the bathroom stall and collapse against the cold metal door.

Why is it whenever I'm near Tysin, it always feels like the rest of the world falls away?

I quickly take care of business and wash my hands. I stare at myself in the mirror and suck in a deep breath, knowing what's waiting for me the moment I walk out.

I release a heavy breath and open the door, coming face-to-face with Tysin.

He's leaning against the wall across from me. His mouth stretches into a slow grin, traveling down my body and stopping on my legs. He drags his lip into his mouth before shaking his head.

"I've never told you how much I love your tattoo," he mutters.

The hallway is dim, the only light coming from the random neon signs scattered sporadically across the walls. He reaches for my hand and tugs me against his body, letting the door close behind me.

He tilts his head down, dragging his nose along the column of my neck.

"You okay?"

He wraps his arms around my waist, taking me by surprise.

"I'm okay …" I trail off. "Better now."

He pulls back, lifting my head to look him in the eyes.

"He'll realize what he's lost."

His gaze softens, searching mine, and I relax against him. Although he doesn't elaborate, I suspect he's saying it because he knows from experience.

The emotion in his voice, the conviction spoken behind his words, says it all.

He traces his thumb over my cheek, brushing his calloused skin over my lower lip. I grip the front of his shirt, my eyes bouncing from his mouth to meet his.

Tension burns between us, and I yearn to kiss him. The thought no more than enters my mind before he leans forward and lightly presses his lips against mine.

I slide my hands up his chest and wrap my arms around his neck. His hand cups my face, tracing his tongue along my lips as I open for him. All I can do is hold on for the ride.

When he breaks the kiss, I pull him back and moan, "Sin," before he crashes his mouth back on mine. This time, it's full of passion and need.

"Fuckkkk, I've missed that sound of your voice," he growls. "Tell me you missed me. Missed this."

"Yessss."

He grips my wrists, pushing my arms above my head, and his mouth dives into my neck. Nipping, sucking, and licking my skin, he makes me squirm beneath him.

"You taste even better than I remember," he adds.

I tug on the strands of his hair. He hitches my leg over his hip and lifts me in his arms, turning to press my back against the wall.

He thrusts into me, grinding his hips over my aching center. I roll my eyes closed, soaking in the rush and the high.

Just like that, everything around us falls away. Nothing exists but him and me.

I've spent the past two years full of anger for what happened between us, hating him for how badly he hurt me.

Yet here we are again.

This will only destroy me in the end, but fuck it if I care.

CHAPTER SEVENTEEN

TYSIN

The sound of her throaty moan when she muttered, "Sin," in my ear played on repeat until we left the arcade.

The guys decided to hit up the clubs while we were out downtown. Trey has been itching to hit up a strip club. He hasn't quit talking about it since we arrived in town.

Originally, I planned to go out with them, but all that changed when I kissed Kyla.

"I think I'm gonna catch a lift back to the hotel," Kyla says, her eyes peering over to mine.

"I'll ride with you," I add.

Madden's brows deepen. "I thought you wanted to go out with us?" he asks, confused.

Kyla's gaze burns into the side of my face. I could feel it without even looking at her.

"I'm trying to cool it on the drinking, is all. Trying to avoid the temptation."

It's not a lie. I'm trying to lay low on the alcohol, which is even harder to do when we're out on the road. The truth is, I've been hitting it hard for the past few years. I need to step back and reel it in, remember what I'm out here to do.

Although, at this moment, I'm not letting myself think too much about right and wrong. All I want is to head back to the hotel with Kyla and get her alone.

Ivy sucks in a sharp breath, sending her into a coughing fit. She smirks when I look over at her, clearly picking up on things. Though if she suspects I want to spend time with Kyla, she's not trying to entice her to stay.

I've been itching to get my hands on her again. Now that I've had a taste, I won't be able to get it off my mind until I do.

When the SUV pulls up outside our hotel, Kyla moves to climb out. She stops to give Ivy a quick hug before she goes, reassuring Madden she's all right.

I follow her, clapping the guys in a handshake.

"Don't get into too much trouble." I raise my brow suggestively, pointing at Trey and Brix before Ivy slugs me.

"Oww!" I shoot my eyes over at her, rubbing my arm.

She shrugs, looking over at Brix, who is cackling.

"You should consider yourself lucky it doesn't hurt more than that too." She flips her hair over her shoulder, effectively ending the conversation. Kyla slaps her hand over her mouth, a giggle slipping out.

"Hey, man, it's not like you haven't had it comin' for a long time," Brix throws out.

"It's been years. Give me a break already," I joke, flipping Ivy the bird before shaking Madden's hand.

"I'll make sure Kyla gets back to her room safely."

"Thanks, man." He nods as I step onto the curb and shut the door behind me.

I follow Kyla through the lobby and into the elevator, appreciating the sight of those legs while imagining them wrapped around my head.

When we make it to her room, she pulls the key card out to unlock it and pushes the door open.

"I'm here. I'm safe." She turns to face me, leaning against the door.

My eyes narrow, dragging my lip through my teeth as I rub my hand over my chin. I stare at her, letting my gaze roam over her body before trailing back to meet hers.

I grip the edge of the doorframe. Her eyes follow the path, her throat bobbing at the sight of my arm flexing.

I have her where I want her, dropping my hands to my side before one darts out to pull her close to me.

She pushes back, earning a low growl.

"Oh, so we're back at this again?"

It's always like this between us.

Push and pull. Want and deny.

I lift her chin to look at me, narrowing my eyes on hers.

This time, she doesn't move or back away. I lean in, her mouth a breath away from mine, our gazes locked.

"Last chance, Kyla."

I give her a second, expecting her to shove me away. I wait a few more for good measure, only it never comes.

When she quirks her brow, I dive in, crashing my lips on hers. She grips the front of my shirt in her fist, pulling me closer.

The sound of her moan slipping from her lips reminds me of the night on the bus. My dick hardens in my pants, begging to be let free. I lean down, hoisting her in my arms, and stalk into her room, letting the door slam shut behind us.

She slips her arms around my neck, grinding against me. It's been so long since I've sunk into her tight pussy. The thought of her mouth wrapped around me has me damn near ready to blow.

But no ... that's not what I'm agonizing over.

The thought of her touching herself on the bus ... and how fucking badly I wanted to watch her and touch her was a slow torture.

I'm out of my mind with need, wanting to taste her. I drop her on the edge of the bed. She falls back, kicking her shoes off in the process.

I step back, leaning against the dresser at the foot of her bed, and pull my shirt over my head.

Her eyes fall on my chest, trailing down to the belt cinched at my waist. She moves to stand before I shake my head.

"Nope," I say with a pop. "Do you know how fucking hard it was for me to picture you in your bed rubbing your fingers over your sweet pussy, knowing I wouldn't get a taste?"

Her breath hitches, her cheeks turning a delicious shade of pink at the mention of that night.

"I want you to take off your clothes and climb up on the bed." I pause, my chest rising and falling fast. I unhook my belt, followed by the button of my jeans. "Only this time. I'm gonna stand here and watch you."

Her eyes flutter, her tongue darting out to trace her lips, but she doesn't move an inch.

"Do it. Now."

She smirks, but she follows my orders. She unbuttons her shorts and pushes them over her hips, letting them drop to the floor.

When I suck in a breath, her eyes peer up at me. She's slow, relishing the way I drink her in and my dick hardens watching her.

I want to reach out and touch her soft skin, but I don't give in.

She's not wearing panties beneath her shorts. The sight of her bare pussy has a growl slipping out of my mouth. It would've been easy for me to touch her back at the arcade.

"Kyla," I mutter sternly.

"I'm going, I'm going." She smiles. "So damn bossy."

"You have no fuckin' idea."

She reaches for her shirt, lifting it over her head before tossing it near her shorts. She's wearing a lace bra, her tits nearly spilling over the top.

Her taut nipples are visible through the thin material. I push my boxer briefs below my hips, squeezing the head of my dick to fend off coming.

She turns, sauntering around the side of the bed.

"Fuck," I grit. "You keep swaying that ass for me, and I'll bury myself deep there first."

Her dark and hungry eyes snap over to mine.

I'm not going to last very long.

She quickly climbs onto the bed and spreads her legs. Her tan skin is a stark contrast to the white sheets.

She dips her hand between them, cupping her pussy, torturing me. The sly grin on her face says she's enjoying it all too much.

I shove my underwear to the floor.

"You want to know how fucking hard it was not to come at the thought of you touching yourself mixed with your soft moans?"

The mention of them filters through my mind, and I grip my dick, thrusting it into my hand. Desire glazes over her eyes as her hand falls away. She gives in, letting me catch a glimpse of her pussy.

She trails her finger up her inner thigh, over her hip, and through her folds. Her pussy glistens before she dips her finger inside again.

Her eyes roll shut, tilting her head back against her pillow.

"Eyes on me, Kyla."

She rolls her head back to look at me. She spreads her pussy lips, and I growl.

"Keep going," she begs me to continue.

I kick off my pants around my ankles and climb up on the foot of the bed. I kneel in front of her and wrap my hand around my dick, brushing my thumb over the sensitive tip.

A bead of precum leaks out, wetting my finger, and I rub it into my skin. Her tongue darts out, wetting her dry lips, and I reach my hand out.

"Open." Her eyes flare before she sucks my finger into her mouth.

I brush my wet finger over her nipple, and she moans. Her hips buck, dragging her hand up to spread her wetness over her clit.

I lie down on my stomach and hold her legs open, trailing my lips along her inner thigh toward her mound. She uses her hand to cover her mouth, and a subtle groan escapes.

"I want to taste you so fucking bad," I growl before flicking my tongue over her swollen bud.

Her legs tremble, clenching tightly around my head, and I grip them in my hands. I suck her clit into my mouth, and she thrusts her hips up to grind against my face.

"Mmm," I moan, vibrating against her pussy. "Fuck my face, baby."

When she comes this time, her legs are wrapped around my head. She tugs on my hair and grinds against my face as if she's fighting for her last breath.

Her body shudders, coming down from the high. I crawl up the bed again, trailing kisses up her stomach and over her breasts.

I trail my tongue over her taut nipple, sucking it into my mouth. She reaches for my head, holding me against her. Her mouth is greedy, her body continuing to thrust up against me.

"More, Tysin," she begs. "I need more."

I lean over her, reaching down between us, and brush the head of my dick through her pussy.

Her eyes soften, and I lift her leg over my shoulder, adjusting the position. She throws her head back and lets out a low moan when I slide inside her tight heat.

"Look at me," I grunt, stopping mid-thrust.

When her eyes meet mine, the smirk she wore on her face earlier is back, sucking the edge of her lip into her mouth.

"Have you thought about us together again?" she asks.

The look on my face must tell her the answer as a grin stretches across her face.

"I want you to fuck my pussy like I've been thinking about for the past two years."

My mouth goes dry, and I piston my hips, hitting her deep.

"My sweet little sinner and her dirty fuckin' mouth." I grunt, pulling out and smacking my dick against her clit.

She stares down, watching me fist my dick while using her juices to slide over me before thrusting back into her.

I lean back on my haunches, pulling her with me so she's on top. Her eyes grow hooded, and she squeezes them shut when she grinds her pussy against me.

I grip her throat. "Look at me," I command.

She slowly blinks her eyes open and wraps her arms around me, kissing me hard. When she pulls back, a salacious smile stretches across her face.

"Ride this dick, baby. Ride it like I've been dreaming about."

CHAPTER EIGHTEEN

KYLA

The sun peeks through the sheer white curtains as I open my eyes before squeezing them shut again. My body goes straight, groaning in agony. Every muscle aches.

What the hell did I do?

When the thought enters my mind, an arm slides over my stomach and pulls me close to them.

Tysin.

He rocks his hips against my ass, pressing a line of kisses across my neck and shoulder. When I arch my back toward him, he sucks in a low hiss and groans.

I'm in bed with Tysin, and we slept together.

I wince, thinking about how lost in the moment I was and how reckless it was for us not to use protection, especially with how things ended before.

Not that it matters this time. I'm on birth control now, and even still, the doctors have told me it'll be difficult for me to conceive if I was to try again down the road.

He tightens his arm around me and whispers, "Good morning," into my ear. Tysin was never much of a cuddler, something that seems to have changed since then.

This isn't me comforting him when he had a bad dream, either. I slipped out of his bed that night before the sun came up, not wanting the guys or Ivy to catch us together.

It's easier to convince myself it didn't mean anything.

Last night, however, I can't say for certain. It certainly didn't feel like it meant nothing.

"Wanna order some breakfast?" he asks.

I force myself not to let the confusion show on my face. The questions swirling in my mind made it impossible to ignore them or think about anything else.

I rub the pads of my fingers over my eyes and yawn, attempting to blink my eyes awake. When I glance over my shoulder at him, he falls back on his pillow. I zero in on his naked body, a white sheet draped over his waist.

Dear Lord. This man is so sexy that it's downright sinful.

He chuckles, my eyes bouncing back up to his face.

"I'm not sure I'm hungry ..." I trail off, moving to climb out of bed.

My clothes are on the other side of the room, so any hope of me doing the walk of shame with my dignity intact is out the window.

Oh well, it's not like this is our first rodeo.

I bend down on the floor, swiping my bra and slip it over my chest, quickly hooking the straps behind my back. His eyes are on me the whole time, tracking my movements. When I finally look up at him, he's fixated on my ass with a sly grin stretching across his face.

I try not to focus on it, but there's no hiding his morning wood growing beneath the thin sheet.

"Why don't you lie back down?" he suggests. "Because I'm starving."

My face warms when I reach down to grab my shorts and slip them on, quickly buttoning them. Tysin's brow furrows, and he sits up straight.

"I think you should go," I mutter, snagging my shirt.

"What's wrong?"

"I just, I think we made a mistake last night."

"Are you kidding me?" His voice changes and all joking disappears.

"No, Tysin, I'm not. We had a good time, an amazing time, but this shouldn't have happened. I literally just ended things with Canon, my fiancé, not even a week ago, and look at us."

He shoves the sheet off him and swings his legs over the edge of the bed. He stalks toward me, not a shred of clothing covering him. He doesn't even try to cover himself up.

It takes everything in me not to look down at him, although I notice out of the corner of my eye just how ready he is for round two.

It doesn't matter how much I want him or how good last night was. I still have no business going down this road again, not with him, not now.

He swipes his boxer briefs and jeans off the floor and quickly pulls them on. He turns to look at me, shaking his head.

The urge to stop him and apologize tugs at my heart, but I ignore it.

We've been on this roller coaster before. I need time to deal with everything being thrown at me. I'm being pulled in two different directions, and what we did last night isn't helping matters.

He doesn't bother to pull his shirt on, gripping it in his fist as he stalks toward me.

For the first time, I get a glimpse at the hurt on his face, and my chest aches as I swallow hard. I don't want to hurt him. Fuck, it's the last thing I ever want to do.

"I want you to look me in the eye and tell me you regret last night."

"Tysin, please."

"Say it." He leans forward to look me in the eyes.

"I'm not doing this with you. You need to go," I grit out, pointing at the door.

"No, I want you to say it. Tell me you regret being with me."

"I think it was a mistake, and it shouldn't have happened."

"Do you regret being with me?"

I clench my jaw, steeling my resolve. "I want you to go."

He shakes his head, dragging his hand through his hair. He's just as conflicted about this as I am.

He stalks toward the door. He reaches his hand out, gripping the handle before he stops. He releases a heavy breath and turns to face me again.

"I deserve this. I know I fuckin' do, but ..." He sighs, shaking his head. "Never mind. It doesn't matter. It never fuckin' mattered."

He hits the door handle, shoving it open, and disappears into the hall, letting the door slam shut behind him.

I manage to drag myself into the shower, letting the hot water relax my aching muscles from the night before. When I make my way downstairs to meet up with the rest of the group for breakfast, Tysin is nowhere to be found.

It's not until we're loading for their show at the Indianapolis Motor Speedway that I finally see him again.

The guys have been amped up for this show all week because they will be performing on the track in front of a packed crowd.

After I punch the address into the GPS and run through the itinerary with Hank, I climb the steps of the bus and collapse on the couch. Brix, Ivy, and Madden are seated at the table, playing a game of cards. Trey disappears into the bathroom, muttering something about fixing his hair.

Tysin, on the other hand, is quiet. He doesn't utter a word, which is unlike him. I'm waiting for Madden or Brix to notice and say something to him.

Any hope we have of getting through the day without incident is out the window when he stomps through the kitchen and slams the door open, swiping a beer.

Madden tosses his cards on the table, losing this round. His jaw ticks at the sight of Tysin.

"What the fuck has gotten into you now?"

Tysin pops the tab, holding the can to his mouth, and chugs the entire thing in one gulp.

He wipes his mouth with the back of his hand, his eyes flashing over to mine. When he catches me looking, he pauses, holding his hand over his mouth. He takes a deep breath and drags his tongue over his lips suggestively.

My face heats at the sight of him, recalling the way he licked his lips after going down on me.

His hair is wet from his shower, so if he's trying to imply he can still taste me, he's doing it to get under my skin.

"What do you mean?" He presses his hand to his chest. His voice turns extra sweet, his attention focusing back on Madden.

"I mean, you were fine last night when we dropped you off at the hotel with Kyla, talking about how you're laying off drinking. Now you're back on some bullshit. What the hell happened between now and then?"

Madden's eyes bounce over to me, and my body goes tense.

He smacks his hands against the table and stands from his seat, walking past Tysin to grab a bottle of water from the fridge.

I clear my throat to get Tysin's attention. My eyes bulge, and I mouth, "What the hell are you doing?"

He rolls his eyes and reaches past Madden for another beer.

"He needs to get laid is his problem." Trey laughs, pushing the door open to the bathroom.

My stomach churns at the thought of Tysin hooking up with someone else.

A slow grin stretches wide across Tysin's face. "Nah, I got some last night."

Trey's face morphs into a laugh, his eyes shooting over to mine. I know exactly what he's thinking, and I shake my head, attempting to convince him otherwise.

What the hell is he doing?

"With who?" Madden asks.

Tysin tosses his empty can in the sink before he pops the tab on his new one, taking another swig.

"Someone I met at the hotel bar," Tysin lies.

My eyes burn into him. I clench my jaw, grating my teeth together. I want so badly to tell him to knock it off.

"The best damn pussy I've ever had too." He groans.

My face warms, and I push myself to my feet, unable to conceal my flush.

He starts laughing, and I shoot my gaze over to his, wishing I could smack the smug look right off his face.

"We always want what we can't have. Ain't that right, Kyla?" He winks, tossing back the rest of his beer.

It takes all my strength not to slam the door behind me, refusing to give away any clues about how Tysin's antics are getting under my skin.

I hit the lock and slouch against the door, sliding down to the floor. I pull my knees up to my chest and rest my head on my folded arms.

As much as he drives me crazy and gets under my skin, I couldn't bring myself to regret being with Tysin.

I don't think I ever could.

CHAPTER NINETEEN

KYLA

"Hey, uhh, Kyla ..." The voice filters through my walkie-talkie.

I blindly reach for the radio, distracted while running through my after-show checklist. The crew is busy stalking back and forth, packing up the equipment and loading it onto the bus parked outside the track.

I unhook the walkie from my hip. "Yes?"

"We have someone up here who's askin' to speak to you. Says his name is Canon."

My eyes widen, and my mouth drops open.

Canon is here?

"I'm wrapping up right now and will be up there in five."

"You got it."

I quickly rush through what's left for me to do. Thankfully, the guys have already gone back to the bus after the show to get cleaned up, leaving me to wrap up everything with the venue.

When I turn the corner outside the track, my eyes land on Canon. Standing off to the side, he's leaning against the wall, his arms crossed in front of him, laughing with one of the security guards.

I suck in a sharp breath at the sight of him. The only thing that's helped get me through this is not having to see him. He's here, standing in front of me, and my heart aches at what we've come to now.

He nods, a broad smile on his face, but when he glances up and sees me, his face brightens, but there's a glimmer of hurt behind his eyes.

You'd never know it if you didn't know him, but I recognize the pain he's carrying with him. I hate knowing how this is tearing him up too, but his decisions brought us here.

His and mine.

"Hi," I say, exhaling a sigh.

"Hey." He grins. He stops his conversation with the security guard and takes a step toward me, wrapping his arms around me in a warm hug.

When he pulls back, he claps the security guard on the back, shaking his hand and thanking him for everything.

"I can't believe you're here right now."

I motion for him to follow me, going around the back of the stadium to give us some privacy.

It's not that I'm not happy to see him—because I am—but I know he has a race tomorrow in Michigan. The fact he's here when he should be on the road causes my anxiety to spike. I can only imagine how ticked his dad will be when he finds out he's here.

"We need to talk, Kyla. We can't keep putting this off."

I nod. He's right. I know it's a lot to ask to keep him waiting until I get home. Every day that passes is slowly torturing me too.

It's hard to find somewhere quiet for us to talk since people from the show tonight are still huddled in groups in the parking lot.

A row of picnic tables lines the back near the concession area. As soon as we round the corner and my eyes land on Tysin, I immediately regret my decision.

"Canon, man, it's good to see you," Madden says when we approach the group.

The guys are standing in a circle. Tysin is smoking a cigarette, and Brix has a beer in his hand. Ivy is next to him, sitting on top of one of the tables. Her legs are hanging over the side, swaying back and forth.

She blinks slowly as the exhaustion from the day sets in. The moment she spots me next to Canon, she perks up, her eyes flying over to mine before glancing over to Tysin and back to me.

I struggle to work up the courage to look at him myself, but the tension in the air is thick. You could cut it with a knife.

The moment I give in and glance his way, my heart aches all over again at the stoic look on his face. His jaw sharp, his eyes emotionless.

My heart is torn between two men. No matter what I do, there's no easy way through this. Someone I care about is going to end up hurt, myself included.

Madden reaches out to shake Canon's hand, pulling him in for a quick hug. I bite my lip as I watch them, wishing the ground would open and swallow me whole.

"Do you think we could get a few minutes alone on the bus before we head out?" I ask, keeping my gaze focused on Madden.

It dawns on me how it may sound or what Tysin could be thinking, so I quickly follow it up with, “We need somewhere to talk for a bit. Privately.”

Tysin coughs, stepping back to reach for a bottle of vodka on the table next to Ivy. He picks it up, unscrews the cap, and takes a heavy swig.

It bothers me he's turning back to drinking. I want to say something to him but now isn't the time. It would only draw attention to something neither of us is ready to talk about right now.

“Yeah, of course.” Madden nods, and Trey steps back, holding his hand out to let us pass.

Trey flashes me a warm smile and a wink. I don't think he has any clue about my past with Tysin, not unless Tysin said something to him, which I highly doubt. He isn't someone who likes to spill his secrets, so anything Trey thinks he knows is because he's observant and has picked up on it.

Despite him and Tysin not getting along in the beginning, they seem to have come around and are getting along better now.

I think they have more in common than either of them cares to admit.

Canon presses his hand to my back once again. This time, the move causes me to flinch.

“You seem worried or on edge. Is everything okay?” Canon asks once we're alone, the door clicking shut behind him as we take the stairs. He crosses his arms in front of his chest, pinning me with a concerned gaze.

“Yeah,” I say, reaching my hand up to rub my fingers over my forehead, massaging my temples. “I have a lot on my mind. I wasn't expecting to see you. Don't get me wrong, I'm happy you're here, but I wish things were different, ya know?”

"You do?" He drops his hands to his side and takes a step toward me.

I hold my hand up, taking a step back to maintain our distance.

He exhales a heavy sigh, and his face falls. I don't know where to go from here, but all I know is I don't see a way back to who we were before the tour began.

"Wish things were different, how?" he asks.

"I wish seeing you felt the same as it did when I boarded the bus ten weeks ago."

He winces, his gaze falling to the floor.

"I guess I deserve to hear that."

"Why were you even with her?" I cut right to the chase.

He sighs, moving across the bus to take a seat on the couch. He stretches his arm along the back, nodding for me to join him. I sit on the opposite end, then turn to face him. I need to look him in the eye when he tells me what I'm about to hear.

"Before the interview with Wired Buzz, where you saw me talking to her outside of my trailer, I need you to know I hadn't talked to her in over a year. It's been almost two years since we split. I told you about our history, both between us and our families. Her brother, Sean, and I have been competing against each other since I was eight."

I nod. It's no secret there's bad blood between their families.

"Our relationship was doomed from the beginning. There was no way her parents or Sean would ever let us be together. No matter what happens between us, there will never be anything more with her. My relationship with Savannah taught me a lot about myself, about what I want in my future, and that's you."

His words are spoken with so much pain and conviction. I want to leap across the couch and into his arms, forgetting everything.

"As much as I want to believe that's true, if I'm what you want in your life, then why'd you kiss her? Why was she pinned against the side of your trailer and again the night at the bar? It makes no sense to me, Canon."

He presses his fingers against the corner of his eyes and shakes his head.

"It was a mistake. One I'll regret for the rest of my life."

Hearing him use the word "mistake" out loud hits me like a ton of bricks, bringing me back to last night with Tysin.

Was being with him a mistake too?

No. No, it wasn't.

Even though it was bad timing and what I was doing was wrong. It would hurt Canon and likely myself again down the road, but everything about being with Tysin felt right.

I couldn't help but feel the same applied for Canon.

If we weren't engaged and their families weren't opposed to them being together, I believe in my heart he would feel differently.

Canon reaches his hand out between us, slipping his fingers into mine.

"I'm sorry," he mumbles.

"I'm sorry too."

It takes a second for the words to sink in, and he asks, "Something happened, didn't it?" His voice cracks. "You're different. I can't explain it."

He swallows hard, squeezing my fingers in his hand as if mustering up the courage to say what he's about to say next.

"It's Tysin, isn't it?"

My body jolts at the mention of his name. I pull my hand back, squeezing it into a fist.

"Why would you think that?"

He chuckles. "I know you, Kyla, better than you think I do. Better than you know yourself sometimes."

I drag my lip between my teeth before pressing them into a firm line.

He deserves to know the truth, too, even if it will hurt him the same way it hurt me.

I nod. "It's not what you think, though."

"It's not what I think?" He laughs, shaking his head.

He lifts his hat off his head, running his fingers over his short hair before pulling it back down again. This time, he pulls the brim low and covers his face.

I release a heavy breath. "Tysin is to me what Savannah is to you."

His eyes dart over to mine, his mouth falling open. "What's that supposed to mean?"

"We have a history. He's my brother's best friend. I didn't think it was ever gonna happen."

"You didn't think telling me this before you went out on the road with him was important? Like, isn't that something I should know?"

He raises his voice, and I wince.

He's right. I should've, but at the time, I didn't believe it mattered. Tysin moved on, almost as if we had never happened. I thought by leaving it in the past, I was doing the same.

"It's not like I was trying to hide anything from you. My relationship with Tysin is complicated. It's not like what you had with Savannah."

"You don't say," he jokes, shaking his head. "Tysin doesn't give a shit about anyone. Did you see the way he spoke to you the day you left? It's no different than any other woman in town. Trust me, I've heard all about it. He uses women and tosses them to the side, just like he'll do to you."

"You don't know what the hell you're talking about," I spit.

I was defending him, even though Canon's right. Tysin has a history of being selfish, and he's done terrible things to me in the past.

Canon pushes himself to stand, pacing back and forth across the small space.

"Will you please sit and talk to me?"

He shakes his head. "I'll talk to you, but I need to stand. I need space for a minute."

He waits for me to continue before motioning with his hand for me to keep going.

"It was two years ago. It was a fling over the summer. As quickly as it began, it was over."

"And you still never thought this was something I should know?"

"I didn't think it mattered. We were engaged, and like you said, I didn't think it meant anything to Tysin."

He crouches down on the floor, pressing his hands against the side of his head as if trying to relieve the pressure.

"He's in love with you," he says before tilting his head back up to look at me.

I fumble over my words, stunned. Now he's just being ridiculous.

I roll my eyes. "Canon, seriously? A second ago, you were reminding me how he treated me like shit. Now you think he loves me?"

"I'm serious." He grits his teeth. "I didn't realize it at the time, but I see it now. He's in love with you. The way he reacted outside, the attitude he had when you left town, even the night at Whiskey Barrel when I proposed."

He winces, folding his hands in front of him and staring down at the floor.

I watch him, waiting for him to speak, letting his words sink in.

I don't think for a second that's how Tysin feels. My mind filters back to the night I let those three words slip. I almost regretted saying it when I did.

It was too quick and happened too fast, but I couldn't take them back because I knew it was how I felt back then. I've been in love with Tysin for as long as I can remember.

For a second, I almost thought it was all a dream. If it weren't for the look that crossed his face, I would've thought it was all in my head.

He didn't say a word and never said it back. All this time, I believed it was because he knew how much it would hurt me to hear him say he didn't feel the same.

Now, here I am, sitting in front of Canon, and he believes Tysin loves me?

"You're wrong."

"Am I?"

I swallow hard, but my throat is dry, making it difficult. I bite down on my lip, a myriad of thoughts swirling through my mind. My head is pounding

"The question is ..." Canon says, his gaze meeting mine. "Do you love him?"

"Canon."

"I deserve to know the truth too."

I grit my teeth, tears filling the brim of my eyes. How could I sit here in front of a man I love, a man who's hurt me but was once the person I wanted to spend the rest of my life with, and tell him I'm still in love with someone else?

How could I say those words when I know it would only hurt him?

We are two fucked-up people in love with people we could never have.

When the barrier gives way and my tears spill over, I nod.

"I do."

There's a glossy look in Canon's eyes. He blinks through it and forces a smile. He presses his hands to his knees and stands, holding his hand out toward me.

I reach out for him, and he pulls me into his arms, wrapping me in a hug. He flips his hat backward and buries his head into my neck.

"I'm sorry for hurting you," he whispers.

Any attempt to keep my emotions in check is gone as tears stream down my face. My body trembles, and the soft sniffle against my ear tells me he's feeling it too.

"I would've fought for you. If I thought you'd forgive me. If I thought it would bring you back to me. I would've fought for you."

"I'm sorry," I mumble. A hiccup slips out, and I slap my hand over my mouth as the emotions wrack through me.

I hate everything about this moment, even though I know it's the right thing to do.

I pull back and reach for the chain hidden beneath the collar of my shirt, where the ring that once held so much hope and promise hangs around my neck. I unhook the clasp and slide it off, staring down at the beautiful diamond.

A tear falls from my eye, and I quickly wipe my face, staring back up at Canon once again.

His eyes are bloodshot, and it breaks my heart to see him like this.

"We both know this ring is meant for someone else."

My lip trembles as I say it, but I attempt to smile when I do. "I hope one day you'll get the love you deserve."

He holds his hand out, taking the ring from me before he folds his hand over mine and pulls me back into a hug.

I couldn't help but think of Tysin at that moment. How can you love someone and want to be with them while still knowing you can't give them what they want?

What they deserve.

You deserve far better than what I could ever give you.

CHAPTER TWENTY

KYLA

“Is there room in here for me?” Ivy asks, poking her head into my bunk.

We’re on the road to the next city. There are no windows in here, so I have no idea what time it is. But if I had to guess, it’s about dinnertime. I haven’t bothered to venture out of my bunk since we hit the road this morning.

I groan, rolling over to pull my eye mask off my face. “Or if you want to get your sorry ass out of bed, you can come crawl into ours, and we can talk about it,” she suggests.

I contemplate it for a moment before deciding to take her up on the offer. The bunk is too small for two people, especially considering I haven’t showered yet today.

She’s a good friend for offering anyway.

"Give me a second, and I'll meet you in there." She nods and pulls the curtain open, sending a ray of sunshine shooting into my eyes.

I wince, collapsing back onto my pillow with a huff. It takes me a second before I finally pull myself together and crawl out.

I stand and stretch, glancing down the hallway. Tysin's seated on the couch, his leg bouncing with his guitar in his hand. He's bent over a piece of paper on the table in front of him, scribbling notes. They've been working on music, tweaking it for their next album. His leg stops when he notices me watching him, his face hard as he stares back at me.

I can't imagine what I look like, so Lord only knows what he thinks when he sees me. I turn, pushing the thought out of my mind, and head into Brix and Ivy's room, shutting the door behind me.

It's been a week since Canon dropped by the show. A week since I returned the ring he gave me. A week since my engagement officially ended.

If I'm being honest, it ended the night I found out he kissed her, but that's not a memory I want to think about again.

I dive onto the bed next to Ivy, whose arm is folded behind her head as she stares up at the TV. An episode of *The Challenge* is playing, and she makes a comment about how CT is fine as hell.

"Don't let Brix hear you." I chuckle, and she laughs.

"How are you?" she asks, reaching for the remote to pause the TV. She rolls over and gives me her full attention.

I turn onto my back, staring up at the ceiling. Ivy has a way of knowing how I'm feeling just by looking at me. I'm still trying to make sense of it all, so the last thing I need is her picking up on things I'm not ready to talk about just yet.

"I'm okay." I sigh. "As good as you can be, I guess, after you call off your engagement and break up with your fiancé."

I laugh, but it's one of those miserable self-deprecating laughs.

"I think seeing him made it harder," I admit. "I felt like I was starting to do better. I expected to have more time, thinking we'd have the conversation when I got back to Carolina Beach. I don't think I was ready to see him even though I know it needed to happen."

"I bet," she says. We sit there in silence for a few minutes.

"What even happened? You still haven't told me."

I exhale, my thoughts swirling as I try to think of where to begin before I finally let it all out. When I'm done, I feel as though I've released ten pounds off my chest, and I'm able to breathe deeper.

"How did you feel when you saw him?"

"Honestly, I knew our relationship was over. It was hard to see him, but I think it hurt more to see his pain than anything. My feelings started to change back when I got the first text message, and I've slowly felt myself pulling away more and more each day."

Ivy nods. "What does this mean for you and Tysin?"

I chuckle slowly before it turns into a groan, throwing my arm over my face. "I don't know."

"You both have been getting close lately. Madden doesn't seem to be catching on, or if he is, he's ignoring it. Who knows? It seems different, though, from the first time you were together."

"It is different. I would be lying if I said our friendship didn't mean a lot to me. The way he's been there for me after the texts has shown me a different side to him. I still have no idea what this means or what he wants."

"Is there any part of you that thinks you'll regret letting Canon go?"

She was asking me the hard questions because she thinks I ended things with Canon for Tysin. I can't lie and say a part of me doesn't hope we can explore what we had between us before, but he isn't the reason.

"No," I say matter-of-factly. "I want to be with a man who knows without a shadow of a doubt he wants to be with me."

The difference between us is that I thought my relationship with Tysin was over because he didn't feel the same way. With Canon, their relationship ended because other people forced them apart.

"I won't ever be a consolation prize for any man."

"Amen, sister!"

I tilt my head over to Ivy and smile.

"If it means anything to you, I don't think it was ever that Tysin didn't have feelings for you."

I sigh. "I know."

I'm starting to believe it more now too. The Tysin I've gotten to see on the tour is different than the one I fell in love with that summer. He's grown and is more mature, even if he still has his old asshole ways.

"I wouldn't have believed it if I hadn't seen it with my own eyes, but watching him pick you up that night and carry you onto the bus, the way he watched you when we went to the arcade, and the pain on his face when he saw you walk up with Canon that night. He plays it off like he doesn't care. He can be a selfish asshole sometimes, but I don't think he wants to hurt you. If I'm being honest, I don't think he ever did."

I curl my arm under my head, tucking my legs up, and stare at a spot on the wall letting her words sink in.

"I guess time will tell."

"You know I'll support you with whatever you decide to do but be careful. I remember how heartbroken you were the first time, and after all you've been through, I'd hate to see you go through it again."

After our chat, I finally pull myself together and force myself off my ass. I can't keep moping around once I've made my decision.

I use the bathroom to wash my face and get cleaned up. I spend some time fixing my hair before pulling it up into a messy bun and adding some makeup.

I keep it light, knowing we're not doing anything too exciting today.

The guys had a few beers while we all played a game of cards. Madden has had a few too many, so when Tysin nods his head toward our bunk, signaling for me to come chat with him, I agree. We both know Madden is too distracted and sucked into their game to pay us any mind.

Tysin climbs into his bunk and scoots over to the side, making room for me to join him. I grin at him, taking a quick glance down the hall to ensure no one is paying attention. Ivy peers over at me, biting the corner of her lip to suppress the grin threatening to break across her face.

Her eyes dart over, and she nods, giving me the all-clear before I press my foot down on my bunk and climb into his. I slap my hand over my mouth to avoid giggling while I scooch my body in and face Tysin.

"Hi." He smiles, folding his arm beneath his head as he turns to look at me.

There's a happiness on his face. I fight the urge to smile like a loon when I realize how happy I feel at this moment.

"Hi," I whisper back, scrunching my face in a smile.

He reaches his hand out, tucking a strand of hair behind my ear. His thumb trails along my cheek, and I suck in a breath from the feel of his hands on me.

My body warms from his touch. When he leans in and presses a soft kiss against my lips, I don't pull back. I don't overthink it or tell myself why this is wrong or too soon.

I relax into him, reaching my hand out to grip his forearm. When his tongue swipes against my mouth, I open up to him, and we tangle our tongues together. I'm swept under, unable to resist the urge to hold back. Butterflies take flight in my stomach, and I moan softly against his lips.

He pulls back an inch, pressing his forehead against mine, and mutters a low, "Fuck," between us.

"I'm sorry for kissing you the moment I finally get you alone, but it's all I've been able to think about."

There's a raw vulnerability in his words. Tysin has always spoken his mind, so to know he's been patient, waiting for me to work through things, hits me in the chest.

"Don't be. I'm the one who's sorry."

His brow furrows.

"You know, the morning after we were together, I told you it was a mistake. I made you believe it shouldn't have happened as if I regretted it."

He holds his hand up and shakes his head. "Don't."

"No." I pull his hand down, and he slips our fingers together. "I need you to know I don't regret it. It's not a mistake. I don't think it was the right time, though. I should've waited until I closed the chapter with Canon."

He nods. "You're right. I think the timing could've been better. I know you, though. I knew you didn't truly think it was a mistake."

My eyes narrow. "Oh yeah?"

He grins. "Yeah." He's silent for a moment before he continues. "Nothing about you and me is ever a mistake."

I release a heavy exhale and close my eyes. He moves his arm from under his head and wraps it around me, pulling me against his chest, all while still holding my hand with the other.

Our bodies melt together, and we lie there, holding each other. Even when we say nothing, I swear it feels like we're saying everything at the same time.

It feels right, and I can't help but believe this is what we both need right now despite all we've gone through.

There's still a niggling fear in the back of my mind. What if it doesn't mean to him what it means to me? I tell myself that's crazy, that I'm overthinking things, but I've been wrong about us before. What if I'm wrong now?

"What are we doing, Tysin?" I ask when I pull back.

"Lying here." He winks.

He must sense the change in my mood when he pulls back. The bunk is starting to get dark as the sun dips below the clouds and the night sky falls over us.

"I want to show you something." He releases my hand and starts reaching for something behind him. It takes him a second, and I move back to give him room.

He reaches into his pocket and pulls out his phone. My eyes widen when I notice the number of unread messages and missed calls, but he doesn't pay them any mind. He clicks on the photos icon, opening an album of photos.

It dawns on me how he doesn't bother to shield the screen as he scrolls through the pictures on his camera roll. Most are of him with the guys or at their shows. There are a few of his guitar and his car parked outside.

My heart drops, though, when his finger lands on a photo I recognize, one I once had saved on my phone. I don't miss the small heart at the bottom, meaning he's saved it as one of his favorites. When he clicks on it, pulling up the picture of the two of us from a day at the beach, I can't hold back the tears that prick my eyes.

"You still have that picture? You saved it?"

It took a while after we went our separate ways before I could bring myself to look at the pictures we took together. I did my best to stay busy, but it wasn't until I was alone in my bed, in the darkness of my room, that the walls around my heart started to crumble.

On the nights when I found myself struggling, I'd pull up those photos and close my eyes, wanting to relive the memories of us together.

Now here I am, lying next to him again.

"I couldn't bring myself to delete it."

I stare up at him, needing to see the look in his eyes. I need to know he's being honest. "This was one of the best days of my life."

I nod. "I used to look at it when I was lying in my bed, missing you."

He tilts my chin up toward him and kisses me.

"After a while, I believed I was only hurting myself more by holding on to them, so I deleted them. At the time, they constantly reminded me of what I lost and would never happen."

When he kisses me again, it's full of passion and need. It's as if he's trying to remove any doubt from my mind. It isn't until what he says next passes his lips that I let myself believe it.

"I'm not going anywhere. You're all I fuckin' want, Kyla. I'll prove it to you this time."

CHAPTER TWENTY-ONE

KYLA

"Holy shit," Ivy mutters as Hank pulls the bus down the long driveway.

"Kyla, you didn't tell us you rented a fucking mansion for the weekend." Madden sounds both excited and pissed.

I glance out the window as we turn into the circular drive and smile when the brick house comes into view.

When I saw the place listed, I almost thought it was too good to be true. The light-colored brick paired with the black iron details gives it a modern medieval vibe.

"It's a damn castle," Brix grunts under his breath.

"Quit your bitching, all of you. You wanted a place to relax for the week. Before you ask, yes, it was within the budget. On the higher end, but within the budget nonetheless."

Madden's chest deflates in relief as if I booked a place for our getaway somewhere that would bank drop them or something.

"The pool and the ATVs are free to use, too. I figured you'd appreciate the relaxation away from people."

I guess that sealed the deal. No one bothered to look back at me or second-guess it from there. Madden smacks Hank on the shoulder, and Brix grabs Ivy by her hips, pulling her into him. He murmurs under his breath how he's ready to get his girl in a swimsuit again.

I knew if they heard the reason I picked it, they'd quickly shut their mouth. Just like that, they were off and out of my hair. It was a win-win for all of us.

Tysin stands in the kitchen of the bus, his arms crossed over his chest, watching me with rapt attention. When I glance over at him, a smirk lines the edge of his mouth. Now that we're finally alone, I'm dying to get his hands on me again.

"What's that look for?"

"Nothin'." He shrugs. "I've been waiting to get you alone for days. We've been crammed in this fuckin' bus forever. Now that I have you alone, I'm not sure I'm ready to go inside."

"Why do you think I booked this place?"

"Ohhh." His eyes light up. "What is it you had in mind?"

"You should see the size of the bedrooms. We practically have an entire wing to ourselves. There's no way anyone would ... eh, hear us."

A slow smile stretches across Tysin's face as he pushes off the counter and saunters toward me.

"You mean to tell me I'm gonna get to fuck you, in a bed, every night for a week?"

I nod. He pushes me against the fridge, gripping my hips, tracing along the hem of my tank top. He dips his hand into my jeans. I tilt my head back, unable to resist the feel of his hands on my body.

The heat of desire in his eyes, mixed with the warmth from his skin, has my body trembling. I reach out, grabbing his forearms to steady myself.

"Do you know how badly I've wanted to get you alone again? How badly I've been dying to taste you?"

His words come out hoarse, need wrapped around every syllable. Hearing him admit he's thought about our first night together has my heart seizing and butterflies taking flight in my stomach.

"How badly?" I ask, pulling back to stare at him.

I need to hear his words, the sound of his voice. Tysin always holds back with me and never lets on how he feels or what he wants.

There were times when I could've sworn, with the way he looked at me, the way he clung to me when we were intimate, his body trembling from my touch—I knew better than to think it was nothing to him. It still doesn't mean I don't question it after how badly he hurt me.

"I'm contemplating taking you back to the room now, bending you over, spreading your ass open, and eating you from behind," he croaks. "The memory of you lying spread open for me plays like a fuckin' movie through my mind, one I can't stop. You consume me."

I run my hand along his neck and pull him close to me, kissing him.

His tongue darts out as his hand skates up my spine. When I open my mouth to him, our tongues tangle together. He nearly takes my breath away, devouring me whole.

He growls, bending down to lift me into his arms. When he grinds his hard length against me, I tilt my head back, and my eyes roll back. Not much separates the two of us, leaving very little to the imagination.

"Tysin," I moan. "Oh my God."

He pulls my top down, attacking my neck. I want to beg him to bend me over the table and fuck me hard. A voice in the back of my head shouts be careful in case Madden or someone were to walk on the bus and catch us, but I can't find it in me to care.

Not anymore.

"Please." I wiggle against him. "Please touch me."

"Fuckkkk." The words are low and full of promise.

He lowers me to the floor and reaches for my hips, spinning me around. He grabs my hands, slamming them against the wall.

"Don't fuckin' move, do you hear me?" he whispers. "I have to make this quick before your brother comes out here and rips my ass to shreds."

I nod, tilting my head back against his shoulder.

I sidestep, widening my stance. "Good girl," he growls.

He slips his hand in the front of my leggings, and I nearly choke on my sharp inhale when he swipes his finger over my clit. I arch my back against him, grinding against the palm of his hand.

"Holy shit, baby, you're so fuckin' wet for me."

I struggle to catch my breath. He dips his hand down farther and mutters for me to open my legs more. His gravelly voice in my ear telling me what to do has me nearly coming before he even gets started.

When his long fingers slip inside me, his thumb rubbing circles over my clit, I have to lock my knees to keep myself from collapsing on the floor.

"Does that feel good, baby?" he asks, reaching his hand up and gripping my hair.

I tilt my head back against him. He nips and bites along my neck.

Tingles spread throughout my body, a telltale sign I'm close. I moan, begging him for more.

"Turn around," he orders, moving me to the edge of the counter in the kitchen. "Put your hands on the counter, and don't you fuckin' move them."

I nod, my breath quivering. There's an urge to disobey him, but that will have to be some other time. Right now, I need him to make me come. Any second now, someone could walk on the bus and catch us.

When he drops to his knees in front of me, it's practically my undoing.

"Tysin." My body shudders.

He reaches for the waistband of my leggings and tugs them down in one swift move, dropping them to the floor. His eyes gleam with desire when he finds my bare pussy wet in front of him.

When he reaches his finger out and lightly brushes it through my folds, I'm ready to flip the tables on him and order him to put me out of my misery.

That is until he speaks again.

"Who does this pussy belong to, Kyla?" His nostrils flare. I move to step out of my pant leg, needing more.

"Tysin, please."

He grits his teeth. "Tell me first, and I will."

"It's yours," I groan, thrusting my hips toward him.

"Who has it always belonged to?"

My breath hitches. "You. Always you."

"That's right, baby. Now reach down and spread your pussy open for me so I can devour you."

I swear on all that's good and holy, there's nothing quite like Tysin's dirty talk.

When his tongue flicks over my clit, his finger swirling around my opening and then slowly entering me, I'm coming before I can say a word.

He curls his finger and buries his face in my pussy, flicking and sucking. It's everything I need, and it takes all my strength to hold my body upright and not collapse on the floor with him.

I squeeze my eyes shut, and stars dance, my body shuddering from the force of my release. When I finally open my eyes a moment later to stare down at him, a satisfied grin stretches across his face.

"Kiss me," he orders. "Taste yourself on my lips."

I lean forward, holding his face in my hands, and kiss him hard with reckless abandon.

He reaches down for my pants and slips them back up my legs, helping me get dressed again. When he finally stands, he wraps his arms around me and pulls me against him.

"We have two more weeks left of the tour," he says, his voice low.

I nod, my head resting on his chest.

"Two more weeks with you. I'd hate for you to feel like I'm pressuring you. Lord knows I don't fuckin' deserve you or this," he admits, his voice raw and gravelly. "We don't know what will happen when the tour wraps up and we both go back to our lives outside this bus. Will you do somethin', though? For me?"

"What is it?"

"Give me this. These next two weeks. Give me this time with you before you leave again."

I think back to how hard it was to walk away from Tysin the last time things didn't work out between us. The thought of us getting close only to lose him scares me, remembering how it destroyed me the last time.

All the nights I cried, wishing I could go back and relive those memories again. Even if that's all I'll have after this is over, I want to hold on to it now.

I'll soak up every second with him like it's my last.

CHAPTER TWENTY-TWO

TYSIN

She's trying to fuckin' kill me.

I grunt, attempting to subtly adjust my dick, hoping like hell no one, certainly not Madden, notices me staring at Kyla.

I peer over at Brix. Judging by his face, he's in the same boat.

Kyla and Ivy have been torturing us all day with these fuckin' TikTok dances. Every time I catch Kyla looking over at me, the way she drags her teeth over her bottom lip, I'm about ready to tell Madden to fuck off and pull his sister down the hallway to my room.

As if the hidden touches and stolen glances in the pool weren't making it hard enough, now I'm stuck sitting in this damn chair watching her in a swimming suit moving her hips in ways I'd love to see with her straddling my lap. Only without a piece of clothing separating us.

“You about done?” Brix groans, his eyes boring into Ivy.

“We’re practicing, babe. We’ve been working on this dance for an hour. We want to get it right.”

“I know how long you’ve been practicing, baby.” He grunts. “I can think of several things we could be practicing, you and me, alone in our fuckin’ room.”

I want to tell Brix to fuck off. He doesn't have to wait until later tonight when everyone is asleep to sneak Ivy into his room. This shit has been like torture.

“Give us three more tries,” she promises, walking across the patio where he’s seated.

Kyla picks up her phone from the tripod, something capturing her attention. Even with the pink highlighting her cheeks from the sun she got today, I notice the blush heating her skin. She presses her lips together, fighting off the smile threatening to break across her face.

Her fingers skate across the screen, typing away before she glances over at me, and my phone vibrates in my pocket.

My eyes never leave hers as I reach for my phone.

Kyla: I can’t wait for everyone to go to bed so you can fuck me in the pool. I want your hands in my hair while you fuck my mouth so hard it makes me gag.

“Motherfucker,” I grunt. My nostrils flare at the visual.

“What?” Madden barks.

“Nothing. It’s nothing,” I retort.

“It sure as hell didn’t sound like nothing,” Trey replies. I want to tell him to shut his fuckin’ mouth. He knows what’s going on between Kyla and me. He’s not stupid.

I’m sure he’d love nothing more than to watch me and Madden have it out.

"I said it's nothing. Drop it."

Madden throws his hands in the air. Brix is too distracted by Ivy to give a shit. Trey, though, he must know something is up when he glances between Kyla and back over at me.

"Mm-hmm." He laughs, adjusting his hat.

Once I know Madden isn't paying attention, I chance a look over at Kyla, and she smiles devilishly at me.

She checks to make sure no one's watching before she mouths, "I promise."

"You better."

She can't message me shit like that, in front of her brother no less, and not follow through. I'm damn near ready to bust through my shorts with how hard I am.

Brix finally lets Ivy go, and they go back to their dancing, leaving us to drool over them. I'm thankful Madden isn't paying attention to what they're doing, or this would be even more difficult.

After their third attempt, they settle on posting that one to their TikTok. Brix doesn't waste any time once she's finished. He's on his feet, pulling her away before he lifts her into his arms and carries her to their room.

"I think I'm gonna settle in for the night too," Madden says, standing to stretch. "I slept like a damn baby last night. It sure as hell beats those small beds on the bus."

Trey doesn't say much. They grab their stuff from the patio table, then head inside, leaving us to follow them.

Once everyone is out of sight, my eyes fall back on Kyla, and I find her staring back at me. She rubs her lips together as she walks slowly toward me.

"You wanna go swimming?" she asks.

"What the fuck do you think? No, I don't want to go swimming. I wanna take you back to my room and bury myself so deep inside you, you'll still feel me tomorrow when you try shakin' your ass in front of me again."

Her chest rises and falls quickly with each strangled breath. "Tysin ..." She drags out.

"You want to go swimming, or do you want me to make that pussy wet?"

Her eyes grow heavy with desire, and fuck, I love seeing how her body responds to me.

"Get in the pool, Kyla."

She reaches for the hem of her tank top and pulls it over her head. She doesn't move from where she stands. Stripping for me, she gives me my own personal show.

Her denim shorts are rolled at her waist, showing the black swimsuit bottoms underneath. They are next to hit the pavement when she pushes them over her hips.

She turns, tiptoeing to the edge of the pool, and grips the metal railing as she steps down into the water before diving in. When she comes back up a few seconds later, she runs her hands through her hair, slicking it back away from her face.

Beads of water fall from her lashes, and she rolls her lips together. All the lights are off inside except the one in the kitchen. It appears everyone has headed to bed, not bothering to make sure we followed them.

I haven't changed out of my trunks from earlier today. I whip off my shirt and dive in, swimming straight for her.

"I think I'm gonna have to spank your ass for that message," I mutter, stalking toward her. Water sloshes around us when I pull her into my arms.

"Why?"

"Do you know how hard it was to hold myself together with your brother sitting across the table from me after reading that shit?"

She giggles. "Oh, I could tell."

I grip her hips, and she sucks in a quick breath, wrapping her legs around my waist. I damn near choke on the groan escaping me.

"What the hell are you doing to me?"

"I don't know, but I like it," she whispers. "I love seeing this side of you."

"You like making me weak over how badly I fucking need you?"

She nods. "I like knowing how much you want me."

"Do you feel this?" I ask, thrusting my hips into her, letting her feel how hard my dick is. It's fighting to break free, begging to be inside her tight heat again.

"Oh God," she moans, her nails dragging into my hair at the base of my neck, gripping it tight as she grinds her pussy against me.

Rope lights hang around the pool's edge, and small wrought-iron lanterns are mounted on the house's exterior. It's the only light we have outside since the sun has long since gone down and the midnight sky has turned black.

I push her against the pool's side and thrust my dick over her center, loving how she trembles in my arms.

I want so badly to reach my hand between us, pull her swimsuit bottoms to the side, and slide inside her tight pussy.

My dick swells more at the thought.

"I want you," she breathes out. "I want you so fuckin' bad, Tysin. Please."

My mouth goes in for the attack, nipping and sucking along her neck. She tilts her head back, resting it along the ledge of the pool.

I pull the top of her swimsuit down. Her tit pops out of her top, and I suck her nipple into my mouth. Her body jolts in my arms, her legs tightening around me. I inhale a sharp breath. I swear, I can feel her pussy hug my dick through the thin material separating us.

I flick my tongue over her nipple, and she continues to rock against me, moaning loudly.

"Sin," she whispers, causing me to growl. "Oh fuck, it feels so good."

When she lazily stares down, watching me, the desire in her eyes mixed with the sight of her dragging her tongue along her lip has me giving in. I need to taste her, all of her.

I can't wait until we're inside. I don't care how risky this is or who could possibly see us.

All that matters is tasting her, consuming her, and making her mine.

I don't care what has happened, who we've been with, or how long we were away from each other. One thing is irrevocably true. Kyla has and always will belong to me. I'm determined to show her no one is meant for her and will love her like I do.

I slip my hands under her arms and hoist her onto the pool's ledge.

"What are you doing?" she asks, her body shuddering. The temperatures outside are stifling, so she can't possibly be cold.

I love knowing her body craves being touched by me.

"Lean back."

She glances at the house before meeting my eyes again.

"Move your ass closer to me and lie back, Kyla. Now."

She tilts her head to the side, her tongue killing me again when she licks her lips. She does what I say and wiggles her ass toward me until she's on the edge, then reclines back to her elbows and stares down at me.

"Mmm, fuck, baby," I moan. "You look fuckin' perfect."

Her body trembles as my fingers skim along her smooth skin, up her legs to where her swimsuit meets the apex of her thighs.

"God, I've thought about having you laid out for me like this all fuckin' day. Watching you dancing in this swimsuit, all I could think about was tasting your sweet pussy."

"Tysin." She exhales harshly, reaching her hand out to run through my hair. I drag my fingers over her thighs, up toward her hips, and pull the strings of her swimsuit, revealing her pussy. I'm about to come at the sight alone.

"You're perfect. Every goddamn inch of you."

I brush the pad of my finger over her clit and watch her body quiver from my touch. Each subtle flick of my finger causes her to moan louder. Her head rolls back before she jolts back, staring down at me again.

"Quit teasing me and lick my pussy."

"Shit." I grit my teeth.

I don't know if I'll be able to get through this without pulling her into the pool, fucking her until neither of us can handle any more.

My tongue slowly laps at her swollen bud. She slips her fingers into my hair, burying my face between her legs. I grip her thighs, holding her to me.

I love teasing her and seeing her body come alive.

Slowly tracing a path down to her entrance, I move back up again, not quite giving her what she wants.

She lifts her ass in the air and pulls my hair, grinding against my face.

"Please," she moans. "Quit teasing me, Tysin. I need you right now."

I chuckle, giving in, and flick my tongue against her clit.

Her body relaxes beneath me, but it's short-lived. Her chest heaves with the force of her heavy breaths. When I use my finger to slowly dip inside her wet heat, she releases a heavy moan.

I curl my finger, brushing along the bundle of nerves. Tremors course through her body, and she sucks in a sharp breath.

"Oh fuckkkk." Her back arches off the ground, and she clutches her legs tightly against the side of my face.

When her body stops trembling and her legs finally release their hold, she rises onto her elbows and stares lazily down at me.

If she thinks I'm going to let her get away with it so easily, she's out of her mind.

"Get over here," I grunt, holding my hand out to her.

She bites her lip and sits up. I lift her into my arms, and she circles her arms around my neck.

My fingers twist into her hair. "I'll never get enough of you."

Her eyes flutter. She reaches between us and positions me at her entrance. I slide into her warm pussy, burying my face into the crook of her neck.

When we finish, this time together, she rolls her eyes closed and sighs my name.

I want nothing more than to be the only name on her lips when she comes.

CHAPTER TWENTY-THREE

TYSIN

"C'mere," I murmur to Kyla, motioning for her to come sit on my lap.

I always loved sitting outside on the patio of our apartment growing up, listening to the rain patter on the ground.

An awning protects us from the heavy rain beating down around us. The humidity is setting in, and the wind is shifting, whistling as it whips through the backyard.

We're taking a break from our first round before I carry her back to my room for more. These nights with her, just the two of us catching up on lost time, is exactly what I've needed the past couple of weeks.

Her hips sway as she saunters toward me. The sight of her thick thighs in her red swimsuit is what dreams are made of.

She takes a seat on my lap, draping her legs across me. I run my hand over her smooth skin up her inner thigh. Even with the rain and thunder rolling in, I still make out the sound of her sharp inhale.

I lean back in the chair, and she wraps her arm around my neck, her head resting on my shoulder.

"What would you do if Madden walked out here and caught us right now?"

"He won't catch us."

"You don't know. You can't say that with certainty," she jokes.

I shrug. "Even if he does, I don't care. It's been a long time coming."

She pulls back, her gaze meeting mine. "You're sure? What if he gets angry with you for keeping it from him?"

"It's not his business, for one. We're both grown adults and can make decisions for ourselves. Not to mention, he has no reason to be."

She nods, not sure if she wants to accept my answer or not. I noticed her hesitancy when we first got here, and I asked her to give me this time.

I think she still struggles with trusting me again, and I can't say I blame her. Especially after how her relationship ended with Canon. Nothing I've done has given her reason to trust it'll be different from two years ago.

"Sometimes I wish you'd tell me what you're thinking," she whispers, moving her head to rest on my shoulder again.

I can't convince her to let me if I don't open up and show her I'm not the same Tysin as before.

"I've noticed I don't have bad dreams when I sleep next to you."

Her body jolts, her head shooting up to look at me. "Really?"

I nod. She knows how to get under my skin like no one else, but she also brings a sense of peace and calmness I've only felt when I'm with her.

"Will you tell me about them?"

I exhale a slow breath and nod. "They're more like flashbacks to nights my mom would bring men home with her or have her friends over. They're all variations of the same, but the worst ones are when she's drunk and passed out, and they'd try to sneak into my room."

Her body tenses. I rub my thumb over her skin to soothe her and remind her she's here with me.

"Is that why you'd come over and stay with us?"

I nod. "There were times they'd come over when I was already in bed. The nights when I was awake and could hear them stumbling through the door, I'd sneak out my bedroom window and make a break for your house. There were times when it happened so frequently, I'd do anything to avoid going home. Some nights, I'd stay with my grandma. I never told her what happened, but she could sense something was off. If I wasn't coming by your house, it was usually because Brix's dad was out of town, and I'd stay at his place."

"Is that why you filed for emancipation when your grandmother passed away?"

"I couldn't do it anymore. She left me her house and money. My mom didn't get a penny. I think it was hard for her to face the truth and take me away from her daughter, but when she passed, she wanted me to be taken care of. I did the only thing I could and got the fuck out of there."

The storm continues to roll through, rain coming down like waves crashing along the shoreline. It reminded me of the ones we'd get back home during hurricane season.

Sometimes I miss being back there—when life was simpler.

"Can I ask you something?" An edge of hesitation is in her words.

She folds her hands against the side of my face, tilting my mouth up to meet hers. The kiss is slow, and it takes everything in me not to carry her into the house, forgetting the serious conversation and focus all my attention on her.

When she pulls back, she keeps her face close to mine, and I nod. "Anything."

She looks down, breaking eye contact before finding mine once again. "You mentioned they'd sneak into your room when she was drunk and passed out. You don't have to tell me. All I want to know is ..." She pauses, her voice breaking. "Did any of them hurt you?"

I grit my teeth, staring past her as I try to find the words. This isn't a conversation I was prepared to have with anyone, much less Kyla.

"You don't have to tell me if you don't want to talk about it. I'll understand."

"I never thought I'd tell anyone about what happened."

She wraps her arms around my neck, hugging me. Even though I haven't told her anything, she must sense what I'm about to share won't be good.

"I've been scared to open up about it. I don't trust people easily, and I don't let people in. It's not something I do. I trust Madden and Brix. I trusted my grandma. Those are the only people I've ever been able to count on."

"You can trust me," she whispers. "I promise it won't change the way I see you or how I feel about you. I'm not going anywhere."

I want to tell her I don't deserve her. To push her away and list all the reasons she's wrong. Remind her of every bad thing I've ever done to hurt her.

"Don't push me away, Tysin. Please. Not again."

"Yeah, baby, they hurt me. What happened to me is the sort of shit that'll haunt your dreams, and I don't want to taint you with those images."

She wraps her arms around my neck. I move her legs to stand, but she doesn't let go. If anything, her hold tightens. Not that I mind one bit. I need her, need to feel her body beneath me, coming alive from my touch.

I bend down and lift her into my arms. She wraps her legs around me, pressing a kiss to my lips, and buries her face in my neck.

"I need you right now," I whisper.

"I know," she adds, her voice low and full of emotion. I don't let myself overthink it.

The animal inside me is awake. It's the one that's turned to sex to fight off the demons lurking in the dark corners of my mind.

I need her to help me forget everything in only the way she can.

When we move past her room, she stops me. "I need to grab something from my room quick, and I'll meet you in yours."

I lower her to the ground, first pinning her to the wall and kissing her hard.

"God, Tysin," she whispers. "I want us to pick up where we left off."

I growl, and she grins. She knows exactly what she's doing to me, and the little temptress will only continue to test me more.

I escape to my room and quickly shed my trunks, jumping in the shower to rinse off. I hear the subtle click of the bedroom door when I step out and pull on a pair of gray sweats, not bothering to wear anything else underneath.

She's sitting on the edge of the bed when I flick the light off to the bathroom, her leg crossed over the other. Her and those fuckin' thighs, I swear all I can think about is having them wrapped around my head, squeezing me tight while I devour her pussy.

I lean against the doorframe, folding my arms over my chest. Her gaze rakes over me. She pauses when her eyes meet the dip of my hips and the obvious bulge growing in my pants.

She's wearing what looks like one of those one-piece swimsuits, but it's not. It's lingerie, made of lace, and I can see her pert nipples peeking through the thin material.

"You're sexy as hell, baby." I moan, unfolding my arms to grip my dick through my pants.

Her eyelids turn heavy, her gaze focusing on my hand before meeting mine.

"Tell me what you want. You want me to fuck you?"

She trails her tongue over her lower lip, running her hand up her thigh. I grit my teeth as I watch her and the salacious grin curving her mouth.

"Kyla," I command. "Tell me. Now. How do you want it, baby?"

She slips off the bed. Each agonizingly slow step toward me makes it hard not to take what I want, but if she wants to tease me, I'll draw it out for her.

When she reaches her hand out to cup my dick through my pants, I know I'm in trouble.

"I want you in my mouth first."

I clench my jaw, my nostrils flaring. I grip her chin in my hand, forcing her eyes to mine. She drags her teeth over her lower lip and smiles devilishly.

"When you smile at me like that, baby, I know we're about to sin."

I brush my palm against the side of her face, and she tilts her head into me, her eyes rolling shut from my touch.

I rub my thumb over her lower lip, and she sucks the tip into her mouth. I inhale a sharp breath, and her eyelids turn heavy with desire.

"Get on your knees, Kyla."

She nods, lowering herself to one knee, then the other. Her long lashes feather along her cheek as she stares up at me. I'm damn near ready to burst at the sight of her.

She's sexy as hell. She reaches her hands up, running them over her chest to cup her breasts before releasing them with a bounce.

I brush my finger along her lip again, and she opens, taking me deep into her mouth. She doesn't take her eyes off me as she does.

I'm waiting for the moment when she gags or pulls back, but fuck me, she continues to taunt me as she takes my finger deeper.

When I pull back, she sucks in a breath and mutters, "Now give me what I really want."

I slip my pants over my hips, staring down at her. Desire glosses her eyes when I fist my dick, thrusting harder, my body going tense with need.

"Tysin," she begs. I take a step closer, brushing the tip along her mouth.

Her tongue darts out, swiping the head of my dick, then sucking me deep. She gags, gripping my thighs before coming back for more.

"Jesus fuckin' Christ," I grunt.

I tangle my fingers in her hair, tugging on the strands, unable to restrain myself anymore.

All this teasing, all fuckin' day, has me going out of my mind. Now she has me in her mouth, and I'm ten seconds away from blowing.

"Fuck, baby, you look so good with my dick in your mouth."

She adds her hand, twisting her wrist while she sucks the tip. I'm unable to keep up.

"I'm 'bout to come, baby. Oh my God, I'm gonna come."

She doesn't pull back, doesn't let up. I don't know if anyone heard me, but I'd be shocked if they didn't.

My knees go weak, my eyes screwing shut with the force of my release.

When I come down from the high, she drags her tongue across her lip as if savoring every drop and has the nerve to hit me with a satisfied smirk.

"Mmm, now that was fuckin' sexy, and it was all for me."

I shake my head, kicking off my pants, my eyes darkening on hers.

"Get on the bed, Kyla. I'm gonna fuck that attitude right out of you."

CHAPTER TWENTY-FOUR

TYSIN

"Fuck, Tysin, you've gotta get up, man," Brix hollers, barging into my bedroom.

Ivy is hot on his heels, her eyes wild and frantic. She looks from me, then over to Kyla before spinning to check down the hallway.

"Are you fuckin' kidding me?" Madden yells.

His voice sends Kyla shooting up in bed, pulling the sheet to cover her chest.

The clock on the nightstand reads after six in the morning. It's still dark outside, but I'm not sure if it's because of the time or the storms that blew through here the night before.

"Oh God," Kyla mumbles under her breath as Madden steps through the doorway. His face is red, his jaw clenched.

He doesn't get upset often, but we all knew he wouldn't be happy if he found out like this.

"You're fuckin' my sister? Behind my back? Are you kiddin' me?"

"Get the hell out of here," I growl.

It's one thing for him to be pissed we kept it from him, but walking in here while we're still in bed, with Kyla naked next to me, is uncalled for.

Ivy steps between us, pressing her hand on Madden's chest. I can't make out what she says under her breath, but it's enough to convince him to storm back out of the room.

When he leaves, I turn toward Brix and Ivy standing at the foot of our bed.

"What the hell happened?" I ask.

"Sorry, man. I tried to get him to chill out, but when he saw you, he was livid."

Saw us? What the hell could he have possibly seen?

"Give us a minute to get dressed, will ya?"

Brix nods. Ivy flashes Kyla a sympathetic look, and Brix reaches for the handle, pulling the door shut behind them.

"Oh God, Tysin. What do we do?"

"I don't know," I mumble. "Brix mentioned he saw something, but I have no clue what he's talking about. Whatever it is, it can't be good."

"Do you think ...?" Kyla stopped, slapping her hand over her mouth.

"Whatever it is, baby, I'll talk to him about it. We'll figure it out. I won't let this get between us, not when he knows the truth."

She runs her hand over her forehead, her eyes downcast, nervously chewing on her lower lip.

I bend down, slipping my sweats over my hips, but don't bother with a T-shirt. It'll have to wait.

She collapses on the edge of the bed, and I lean down to press a kiss on her lips.

“You should get up and get dressed. You can grab a shirt and shorts from my suitcase if you need to.”

We hadn’t expected to sleep this late. She’s been sneaking out before the sun is up for a while.

We knew, sooner or later, it was all going to come to an end. Madden would find out eventually. We’ve been getting away with this behind his back for far too long.

“I’m gonna go talk to Madden,” I say, kissing her again.

I slip out of the room, not bothering to wait while she gets dressed.

The last thing I need is to get distracted at the sight of her crawling out of bed and risk him walking in on us again.

Madden is leaning against the counter when I stalk into the kitchen. One hand grips the edge of the marble, the other holding his coffee, while he stares absentmindedly at the floor.

Brix and Ivy are seated at the bar, eyes wide like they are on pins and needles. Brix’s gaze bounces over to me. He raises his brow and gives me a quick headshake.

Ivy’s hand rubbing Brix’s back stops when she sees me. The look on her face is more reassuring than his.

“Want to tell me what the hell is going on?” I ask.

“I should ask you the same thing,” Madden retorts. “What the hell is happening between you and my sister? Is this the reason she called off her engagement?”

“What? No!” I widen my stance, crossing my arms over my chest. “Canon was messing around with his ex back home. He fucked it up between them all on his own.”

“Then explain to me why when I woke up this morning to find the yard ripped apart from the storm, I checked the surveillance cameras to see what happened last night and found you with my sister.” He shakes his head, waving his hand toward the pool.

Ah, fuck.

We were too busy worrying about being quiet or trying to be anyway. We never stopped to consider if there were cameras around. Not to mention, you wouldn't think they'd leave the access to them to the tenants while they stayed here, either.

"It's not what it looks like, Madden. I swear."

"Well, explain it to me because it sounds like you're back to your bullshit. You can sleep your way through CB, but you don't have to drag my sister into your fuckin' problems."

"Oh, whoa, whoa!" Brix says, circling the counter.

It was a cheap shot, a low blow designed to hurt me, even if it is true.

"It's not what you think, man. You need to calm down and give him a chance to explain," Brix defends.

The room turns silent when Trey comes waltzing into the kitchen. He walks between us to grab a bowl and spoon before opening the fridge for a carton of milk.

"Everything okay?" he asks, dropping his spoon into the bowl. His eyes bounce from me over to Madden before landing on Brix.

"Did you know?" Madden asks Trey.

His brow furrows in confusion, reaching for the cereal box on the counter. He flips the top and proceeds to pour some into his bowl.

"Do I know what?" Trey asks.

"Well, everyone else here seems to know about Tysin and Kyla, except for me."

"I don't know anything," Trey says. We both know it's a lie. The first day we left on tour, he picked up on the fact Kyla and I have history.

"How long has it been going on? How is it they know, but I have no idea?" Madden waves his hand over to Brix and Ivy.

Ivy presses her lips together, staring down at the counter. She could speak up and tell Madden the truth. I wouldn't blame her after what happened with the bet. She deserves to get me back for coming between the two of them.

"It started two summers ago," I say, wincing. It wasn't going to help matters, but he wanted to know, and it was time he heard the truth.

"Two summers ago?" he says with a laugh before his face drops. There's a flicker of apprehension on Ivy's face. She steps between us, turning to face Madden.

"I told you it's not what you think, Madd."

"Madden, I think you should talk to your sister." Ivy tries to deflect it from me. She seems concerned about my admission.

"Two years ago?" he mumbles, looking from Ivy and back to me. "It was you, wasn't it? You're the reason ..." His voice drifts off.

Ivy holds her hand up between us, stopping him from continuing, and his eyes flash around the room.

"I know what you're gonna say, Madden, but it's not your place," Ivy reasons.

My nostrils flare, and my shoulders tense as I take a deep breath to calm my erratic pulse.

"I've never seen you treat a woman with respect in all our time as friends. Two years ago?" He huffs. "Two years ago, I watched my sister go through the most unimaginable pain, and I never knew you were the person behind it all. I made a promise to stay by her side, and I did, but if I'd known it was you who hurt her, it would've changed everything."

I hang my head, hating to admit it, but he's right. I hurt her, and he has every right to be mad at me.

"I never wanted to hurt her. She's not like all the others. Okay? You have to believe me. It's different with her."

He laughs, shaking his head. "If that's true, then why didn't you tell me about it two years ago? Why did she move on and get engaged to Canon?"

"I fucked up, man."

He chuckles as if saying, *Tell me I didn't already call it.*

"I fucked up, and I let her go for this exact reason. The exact reason you're standing here, with that smirk on your face and this bullshit assumption about the type of man I am. I let that shit get to my head." I pound my finger against my temple. "I know I don't deserve her. You think I haven't known it for years? You think I haven't let that shit torment me?"

"Hey, hey." Brix wraps his arms around me and pushes me back, trying to calm me down. "It's gonna be okay, man. Stay calm," he mutters under his breath.

Trey stands in the corner and casually takes a bite of his cereal, watching it all go down. Madden shakes his head, waving me off, and takes off toward the patio door.

"No, man. No, you want to hear the truth, then stay the fuck put and hear it," I growl.

He stops and shakes his head. His jaw set, his eyes narrowing in frustration.

"I know I hurt her when I let her go, but it was because I believed I'd never be good enough for her. I still don't deserve her. Maybe it makes me selfish, call me an asshole all you want, but I'm not letting her go this time. Not again."

I rake my teeth over my lower lip, pacing back and forth.

"I'm not going to let you come between us, Madd. I'm not. I love her. You hear me? I fuckin' love her, so don't come at me, acting like you know anything. You don't know shit about us. Not even a little bit. I'd walk through fire for that woman, and I'm done running away from this and from her."

The strangled sob coming from behind me jolts me out of my anger-fueled stare down. At first, I think it's coming from Ivy. Tears well up in her eyes, and she nods behind me, flashing me a sympathetic smile.

"You love me?" Kyla croaks, and I spin around, finding her arm wrapped around her waist and the other covering her mouth. Tears spill from her eyes, and her body trembles.

"C'mere, baby," I whisper, reaching out to pull her against me.

I don't bother sticking around. I bend down to pick her up and carry her in my arms back to my room. I never thought I'd see the day when I'd say those words, and I certainly hadn't expected it to go down the way it did.

We're two steps down the hall when I hear Trey say, "Hey, man, I think you should know Tysin is seeing your sister." He laughs. "I just found out but thought you should know."

Kyla buries her face in my neck and giggles, wrapping her legs around my waist.

"He's a jackass," I grunt.

As soon as we reach my room, I cross the space toward the bathroom. I hit the lock behind me, not wanting to deal with any of these fuckers walking in on us again.

"Shower with me," I whisper, lowering her to the floor.

She nods as I bend down, pressing a kiss to her lips. I reach for the hem of my shirt to pull it over her head. She follows suit, slipping my shorts she's wearing over her hips. The sight of her has me grinning ear to ear.

She turns on the water, never taking her eyes off me as I quickly shed my sweats. I slip my arm around her waist, carrying her into the shower. Her yelp turns into a giggle as she tilts her head back beneath the spray.

"Tysin." She releases her legs from around me to stand. I tilt her chin to look me in the eyes, water streaming down her face.

"Kyla," I reply, staring into her eyes. I hope she knows how much these words mean to me. "I love you."

She sighs, her eyes falling closed. She presses her lips together to fight off the urge to smile, but there's no holding back the grin breaking across her face.

"Say it again," she urges. "Please. I want to hear you say it again."

"I love you, Kyla."

She grips the back of my neck, and I crash my lips against hers.

When she pulls back, she stares up at me, and all I see is love shining back in her gaze. It's a love I've never felt before and certainly never thought I'd be lucky enough to have.

I don't know if I'll ever feel worthy of her, but nothing can top this feeling right now.

"I love you too," she whispers.

When I lift her into my arms and pin her against the wall, thrusting into her, it's different this time. The look in her eyes and the emotions surging through me are unmatched.

I'm making love to her, and I want to keep loving her for the rest of my life.

CHAPTER TWENTY-FIVE

TYSIN

"Thank God," I mumble, walking into the kitchen the following morning to find coffee brewing. I take a deep breath, inhaling the familiar aroma.

Ivy is the only one who drinks coffee other than me. She must've known I'd be needing it after the last twenty-four hours.

I pour some into the last cup hanging from the coffee bar, reading, "I like my coffee black like my heart." I smirk, suspecting Ivy saved it for me. I lift the cup to my lips, glancing out the window to the patio, and spot Madden sitting in a lawn chair facing the pool.

After our argument yesterday, Kyla and I kept our distance and hung out in my room. The secret was out, which meant we didn't have to worry about sneaking around anymore.

I circle the bar and open the sliding glass door. Madden's gaze snaps over to me, checking to see who it is. He exhales harshly, lifting his arm over his eyes.

"We need to talk."

There are no mincing words with him anymore.

He'll have to come around eventually because I'm not giving up or walking away from Kyla again. I certainly am not going to play this game where we walk on eggshells around each other.

We have a few more shows before we wrap up our tour and head back to North Carolina. We've been best friends for far too long to be arguing over shit he has no business sticking his nose into or being mad about. Not anymore.

I want to be with Kyla. I don't want to hurt her.

"You should know, I can't think of anyone I'd want to end up with my sister more than you," Madden says when I take a seat next to him.

His admission shocks the hell out of me. What the heck is he pissed off for then?

"I've watched how you treat women, though, Tysin. I was there when you and Brix made the bet about Ivy. I've seen all the women you've brought home with you from Whiskey Barrel or any other show we've played. You have to understand it from my perspective, man. She's my fuckin' sister."

He leans forward, moving his legs to the ground. He rests his elbows on his knees, folding his hands together. It's almost like he's gearing up for an argument.

If he wants a fight, he's not gonna get one with me.

"I should've told you how I felt before it got to this point. You shouldn't have had to find out the way you did. To be fair, though, there wasn't anything to tell until recently."

He shakes his head, rubbing his fingers over his forehead, then drops his hands to stare at me.

"She was engaged to Canon only a few weeks ago, and she was happy. You can't tell me this wasn't because of you."

"I never meant to come between the two of them. He fucked it up all on his own. I won't lie to you, though. As soon as shit went down, I wasn't gonna hold myself back anymore. I let her go once before. I won't do it again."

"So it was you?"

I tilt my chin down in guilt, remembering the hurt in her eyes the night she stormed out of my house and my life.

"Two years ago, the summer Brix and Ivy started dating, we started seeing each other. I fucked it up, Madden. I hurt her, and not a day has gone by since when it hasn't eaten me up inside. We both know I wasn't in a place to be with someone, certainly not a woman like her. Even sitting here today, I still question if I deserve her."

"Then why can't you let her go and move on?"

"I have once." I wince, thinking back to all the nights I used alcohol to numb the pain and blur her face out of my memory. "I tried to let her go. I thought I was doing what was best for her and our friendship."

"I remember how she was that summer. I saw the change in her, I watched her battle the demons, and she never would tell me what happened. She wouldn't tell me who hurt her, but I stood next to her and helped her. Now you're sitting here telling me all of this. What's changed?"

The guilt rising in my throat burns. "I made a mistake. The biggest fuckin' mistake of my life."

I don't know if it's the torment in my voice or the look on my face, but he believes me.

We've never been the type to open up about feelings and shit, so the fact I'm doing it now speaks for itself.

"I didn't think I could offer her anything. She deserves someone like Canon, who could give her the life she wants. The house, the marriage, and the kids. We both know I didn't grow up in a loving home. I don't think I'm made for that life ..."

He clenches his jaw and nods. It's written on his face, plain as day. He wants to scream at me, *Then why are you fucking around with her if you're only gonna hurt her?*

"But I want to be." I finish.

Silence falls over us before I open up and spill it all, starting from the beginning. I tell him about how I walked into Breaking Waves that day, looking for her boss, Garrett. He owns the small surf shop and has a few close friends who work on and ride motorcycles.

I was only there to see if he could hook me up with them and help me out with some work I needed done on mine.

He clenched his jaw when I told him about how we snuck around behind his back, spending time together, just the two of us.

"She's been there for me." I lift my coffee to my lips, then set it on the table next to us. "You know, the nights when I'd sneak over and needed a place to stay, she was always there. She was like an angel standing at the door, there to save me. She let me in."

He smiles. "I promise, I'm not gonna stand between the two of you. I think there's a lot you need to talk about and work through. There are things you still don't know, and if you did, I think you'd understand why I reacted the way I did."

I swallow hard, wondering what it could be. "Either way, I trust Kyla. She has a good head on her shoulders, and she's always been someone who knows what she wants. When she sets her eye on something, she won't give up. I won't be the one to stand in the way of her happiness."

I reach my hand out to him, and he claps it, pulling me toward him in a hug.

When we sit back, he drops his smile and sighs heavily. "There's something I've been keeping from you for a while that I need to tell you about too."

He presses his lips together, and I narrow my gaze. Whatever he's about to say, we both know I'm not going to like it.

"Your mom called my parents' house before we left on tour. She was looking for me and asked them to relay a message in hopes I'd have you call her."

I grit my teeth. Anger coils in my stomach, and I clench my hands into fists.

"Did you call her back?"

He nods. "I figured something had to be up if she went through all the trouble to reach me. She gave my mom some story about how she's going through a hard time. I figured she was looking for a handout, so I called her myself."

My brows shoot up. Madden isn't one to go digging into other people's business, so the fact he did it surprises the hell out of me.

"Listen, I know you've never told me about all the shit she put you through growing up. It wasn't my place to get involved. If you think we didn't notice, though, you're out of your damn mind. Man, I remember the time she left you outside the gas station by yourself all because you asked her to buy you food. You remember that shit?"

I nod. It wasn't the first time she pulled a stunt like that, either.

That day was a rough one, though. It was after the second time Child Protective Services showed up at our door. I never knew for certain, but she always believed it was our neighbor across the hall reporting her for neglect. She'd leave me home for hours by myself with nothing in the cupboards to eat but scraps.

She dragged me to the gas station that day, not wanting to leave me alone again. She was desperate to get her liquor and a pack of cigarettes and ordered me to keep my mouth shut when we were in the store.

When I asked her for something to eat in front of the gas station attendant, she slapped me across my face and pulled me out the door by the collar of my shirt, forcing me to walk home by myself.

Thankfully, before I left, the woman behind the counter was nice enough to offer me a sandwich and a bag of chips while I waited for Madden and his mom to arrive.

She was always pulling the same old shit, even now.

"You didn't give her a penny, did you?"

He nods slowly.

"Are you fuckin' kidding me? How much?"

"Twenty grand."

I push myself to stand, hitting the table causing my coffee to slosh over the edge.

"What the hell were you thinking?" I growl.

"Twenty grand, paid out monthly over the next three years, to leave you alone and not come back."

"What do you mean?"

"I paid her off to keep her mouth shut."

I release a slow breath and shake my head, forcing myself to sit back down. I stare at my hands, not sure what to say.

"She's always been selfish and unpredictable. We've worked hard to get to where we are now. I made her sign a contract before she ever saw a penny. I knew if she took the money, it would be better off this way."

My nostrils flare, and I swallow the emotion rising in my throat

"I'm sorry," he croaks. "I should've told you. I don't blame you for being angry. I'm pissed at myself, but I promise I only did it to protect you."

"I guess we've both been keeping our share of secrets, huh?"

He sighs. "Yeah, I guess you're right."

Silence falls over us, and I pick up my coffee to finish what's left. We both stare out into the yard. The storm that blew through here flipped over one of the tables on the other side of the patio, causing glass to shatter everywhere.

When Brix woke us up, he mentioned Madden was awake, checking the cameras from the night before to see what had happened.

I guess he found more than he bargained for.

"So, you love her?" His voice cuts through the quietness.

I think about yesterday and my admission to him. I never thought the day would come when I'd say those words out loud to anyone. My mom never told me she loved me, and even when my grandma was alive, she wasn't someone who expressed her feelings in words, although I don't doubt she did.

"I do."

He smiles, and it's a genuine smile. "It should go without saying, but if you hurt her again, I'll hurt you."

"I'd take a bullet before I'd ever want to hurt her again."

"You really mean it, don't you?"

I nod. "Yeah, I do. I've spent too much fuckin' time denying my feelings, telling myself I'd never deserve her. I want to be worthy of her, though, and I want to prove to her I can be."

He pushes himself to stand, and I do the same. He pulls me in for a hug.

"I'm happy for you, man. You deserve to be happy, to find the kind of love I know Kyla has for you."

"Thanks," I say, trying to force down the emotions his words stir in me.

Madden has always been my family, both he and Brix. They're all I've had since my grandma passed away.

One day, I hope we can make it official.

CHAPTER TWENTY-SIX

TYSIN

After my conversation with Madden, I walk down near the pond at the back of the property and take a seat at the end of the dock.

I'm not surprised to hear how my mom was back to going to any length she could to get money, taking it as far as reaching out to Kyla and Madden's parents.

I've had her number blocked for months now. She must've realized after her calls and messages went unanswered.

"You want some company?" Brix asks.

I lift my hand up to shield my eyes from the piercing rays beaming down on us and nod. "Go for it."

He takes the spot next to me. We sit quietly, staring out onto the water. It's peaceful, with the sound of cicadas and birds chirping around us in the distance.

You couldn't sit outside and enjoy the sounds of nature where I lived growing up. If my mom wasn't shouting at me, it was one of the neighbors or the familiar sound of emergency sirens nearby.

The only time I escaped the chaos was when I went down by the water and listened to the waves lapping at the shoreline. Although after things ended with Kyla, I found myself going down there less and less.

I guess it reminded me too much of her.

"How'd your conversation with Madden go?" Brix asks after the silence ticks by.

I shrug. "Better than expected. I'm putting off talking to Kyla, though. We have a lot to talk about, a lot I need to own up to if I want us to have a relationship, and I don't have the slightest clue where to begin."

"It's not something you can fix overnight." Brix tilts his head to the side. He reaches into the bucket sitting at the end of the dock and tosses food pellets into the water. The fish swim in a frenzy to eat every last bite.

"How did you convince Ivy to forgive you?" I lean forward, resting my forearms on my knees.

"Time. Effort. She needed to hear me own up to my mistakes and admit where I was wrong. After that, though, you just have to prove to her you're not going anywhere. I woke up every day and showed her I was willing to fight for her and earn her trust back."

I nod. He's right. I've given her every reason not to trust me. I've pushed her away more times than I can count. I can't say everything she wants to hear and expect her to believe me.

She needs me to step up and be the man she deserves.

"I think I'm just scared, man." I croak. "What if I let her in and she realizes I'm not who she wants? Every person in my life, except for you and Madden, has either used me or chosen not to stick around. What if she leaves too?"

Brix swallows and shrugs. "What if she doesn't?" He squints, turning his head to face me. "What if you've been pushing her away when she was the person sent to you to prove you deserve more than hookups and one-night stands?"

"Look at you." I chuckle. "Ivy took your balls and turned you into a fuckin' philosopher."

He tosses the rest of the pellets in his hand into the water and shoves me, nearly sending me falling into the water too.

"I'm serious, man. I've lived that life, and I know where you've been. Going to shows, taking home random chicks. Don't get me wrong, there were some fun times, but it was meaningless. Empty."

"Nothing was fulfilling about the life I was living. It was brutal waking up the next morning after she took off out of town. If I thought the life I was living before was low, I hit the bottom of the fuckin' well. I couldn't live without her, but more importantly, I didn't want to. I had to fight for her, though, fight to earn her trust. That's what she deserves, Tysin."

He has a point. For the past two years, since Kyla took off out of my life, I've just been going through the motions. Walking around numb, turning to alcohol and meaningless sex to fulfill the ache she left in my chest.

I may not be the man she deserves on paper, but no one could love her as much as I do. I've already stood by and watched her with someone else. I don't want to let her go and do it ever again.

"Can I tell you something?" Brix asks.

"Of course." My brow deepens, not sure where this could be going.

"I'm gonna propose to Ivy."

My eyes nearly bulge out of their sockets. "Holy. Shit."

He grins and nods. "Right? Who would've ever fuckin' thought?"

"Not me." I cackle.

He elbows me in the side and shakes his head.

"I know we're young and all this shit, but I want to spend the rest of my life with her. She's it for me, man. I want to have a house and a family with her, all of it. What's the point of any of this, the money, fame, and success, if you can't enjoy it with the people you love?"

No amount of money in the world could fill the pit of emptiness of being alone. If I've learned one thing since signing with our record label, it's that people will take advantage of you, and it's hard to find the ones you can trust.

Kyla has always been there for me, for us. She's never given me a reason to question where she stood or what she wanted.

"Congratulations, man. I'm fuckin' stoked for both of you. Do you have any plans for when and where?"

He shrugs. "I have no clue. I want it to be big. Epic. I'm still trying to figure out all the details, but I was thinking at one of our last shows."

"I'm happy for you both. You deserve it too, ya know?"

He nods, his mouth curling up in a smile. "Yeah, you deserve this too."

We both turn back toward the water.

Who would've thought when the tour began we'd end up here? I always thought when we hit the road that we'd be partying every night, showing up at the venue hungover ready for another round.

Guess life has another plan in store for us.

"I think I'm gonna go talk to her." I sigh, pushing myself to stand.

I extend my hand out toward Brix, helping him up. He pulls me in for a hug, clapping me on the back.

"Good luck, man. She loves you. I don't know what the hell she sees in ya, but she does," he jokes, and I push him. He nearly falls over the edge of the dock into the water.

He stumbles and throws his head back, laughing.

Ivy's standing on the patio when we head back up the hill toward the house. Her arms are crossed, and she's wearing a smirk.

"Did the boys do some bonding?" She snickers.

"We did." Brix laughs, tugging her into his arms. "Now it's time for the two of us to head inside and do a little bonding of our own."

She rolls her eyes and pushes him away. "He's always had his way with the ladies." Ivy throws her thumb at Brix, turning to pull the screen door open. "A real sweet talker."

Brix lifts her into his arms. She giggles, begging him to put her down as he takes off down the hallway.

Kyla sits at the vanity, her silk robe wrapped around her waist. Her hair is up in what I've recently learned are pin curls. The black drapes are open, the sunlight streaming in. Her phone is beside her on the table, blaring one of our earlier songs.

She doesn't notice me at first, so I lean against the doorframe and take her in. Her legs are crossed beneath her, showing off her smooth tan skin. My fingers and lips tingle, wanting to lick and touch every inch.

I clear my throat, and she jolts. Glancing over her shoulder, she smiles when she sees me.

"How long have you been standing there?"

I shrug. "A few minutes."

She drags her teeth over her lip and grins, spinning her chair around to face me.

"How'd your talk with Madden go?"

I step into the room and push the door shut behind me. Her face falls, worry casting shadows on her features when she stares down at the floor.

"It went well. Gave me a lot to think about, so I went down by the pond for a bit and talked with Brix."

She tilts her head up. "Okay."

The word hangs in the air. I can sense in her posture, her shoulders pulled tight and the frown lines on her face that she's not sure what to think.

I bend down on my knee, and she sucks in a breath, her eyes widening. I chuckle, pulling her on the floor with me and into my lap. She straddles me, circling her arms around my neck.

"Need to feel you," I murmur against her neck as I kiss her.

She drags her nails through my hair, tilting my head back. "Now's not the time to seduce me. Get to talkin', Briggs."

I grin, pressing a quick kiss against her lips, and nod.

"Madden reminded me how much I hurt you after things ended before. I didn't realize he knew about us, or at least suspected you were seeing someone and were struggling after things ended."

"He's my brother. After a while, I couldn't hide it from him anymore." She swallows hard. "He figured out something happened. I never told him who and insisted it didn't matter. I didn't want it to come between the two of you, especially when there was no point anyway."

I nod, staring past her, thinking back to the pain in her eyes the last time I saw her that summer. It's stayed with me, the visual clear as day in my memory.

"There's more, though, Tysin. More I haven't told you."

My brow deepens, turning back to meet her gaze. She chews on her lip as if considering her next words.

"Kyla," I whisper. "What is it?"

She moves to slide off my lap, and I tighten my arms around her.

"Please, whatever it is ... I'm not going anywhere. Just don't leave. I need to hold you right now."

Tears well up in her eyes, and she quickly brushes them away, turning to stare out the window. My heart aches, thoughts racing through my mind.

I don't know what it is, but I can feel it. I can sense in my bones that whatever she's about to say will change everything between us.

She takes a deep breath and turns back toward me, tucking the strand of hair falling from her curls behind her ear.

"Tysin, I was pregnant."

Pregnant.

She was pregnant.

What does she mean by *was*?

I don't hear anything else outside of the sound of my blood pumping through me. My heart beats so fast that I expect it to hammer right out of my chest.

She presses her palms against the side of my face, brushing her thumb over my cheek.

"Tysin," she repeats, almost as if she's trying to shake me awake. "Will you please say something?"

"Pregnant?" I mutter. "You're pregnant? You were pregnant?"

She looks down, folding her hand over her mouth, unable to hold back the emotion anymore.

I have so many questions, but I can't even form a sentence.

I tighten my arms around her, crushing her body against mine, and bury my nose into her neck. When a sob slips out of her mouth, there's no stopping the tears from spilling over.

I don't remember the last time I cried. I didn't even shed a tear at my grandma's funeral.

I'd give anything, though, if I could take away her pain, even if it meant breaking my heart in the process.

CHAPTER TWENTY-SEVEN

KYLA

I've bottled this up inside for so long, so when I finally said those words, it was like a dam broke, and the tears spilled out of me.

"I found out I was pregnant the morning after we came out to Vibrate to watch you open for High Octane."

There's a flicker in Tysin's eyes, and I know he's piecing it all together.

Brix was persistent about winning Ivy back after she found out about the bet. He was relentless and eventually wore me down. I was already hanging on by a thread, and I knew Ivy was heartbroken about what happened with them.

After talking with Brix, we made plans to convince Ivy to come out with us in hopes if she saw him, maybe she'd give him a chance and at least hear him out.

"I hadn't been feeling well the day of the concert. I spent most of it curled up on the couch. I knew Ivy needed me as much as I needed to be with her, so I pulled myself together, and we went out to the show."

This was the only time I saw Tysin at one of their shows after he broke things off with me.

"I woke up the next morning in excruciating pain. I could barely stand long enough to go to the bathroom. I only made it a few steps before curling up on the floor in a ball, unable to move. That's where Madden found me."

His lips part before snapping shut, and he swallows hard. He brushes his thumb over my lower back, attempting to console me. Tears are filling his eyes again, likely anticipating where the story is going.

"He picked me up off the floor and carried me out of there to the hospital. I didn't even realize how much blood I'd lost until I got there, and they immediately wheeled me back.

"It's hard to describe. On the one hand, it felt like every second ticked by in slow motion, but on the other, the words were out of their mouths before I had a chance to fully digest what they were saying."

Tysin reaches his hand up, folding it against the side of my face, and brushes a tear away from my eye.

"The doctor came in after giving me an ultrasound and told me I was suffering an ectopic pregnancy. Apparently, I had been lucky because if I had waited even another thirty minutes, it could've been far worse.

"I remember looking at her thinking, how could you sit here and tell me I'm lucky? What about telling me I'm pregnant and I'm miscarrying in one breath makes you believe for a second I'm lucky?"

Tysin winces, leaning in to press a kiss to the base of my neck, his arms tightening around me.

I need to get this out, so I continue.

"I refused to tell Madden who the father was because I knew if he found out it was yours, and the truth about where our relationship was, it would tear your friendship apart. I didn't want to do that to you or to him, even if I tried to convince myself I hated you for what happened."

"Madden was there for me through it all, though. You have to understand that's where his anger comes from. I don't think for a second he doesn't want us to be together or believes you wouldn't be good for me. He saw me in the lowest point of my life, and because Ivy wasn't around, he was the one who helped me through it."

There's a flicker of understanding in his eyes, and he nods.

Tears trail down his face, and my heart aches, wondering what he must be thinking. It's a lot to lay on him, and a part of me worries this could push him away again.

"He lied to my parents, made up a story about me staying down at Brix's beach house for the week while I was in the hospital. He took care of the bill, so they never knew anything. He was my hero that day, and when he asked me to do him a favor and join you guys on the road, I couldn't say no. Even if I knew it would make you mad being around me again, I felt like I owed him for all he went through to take care of me."

Tysin lifts his hand to cup my face and brushes his thumb over my lip. He leans in, pressing his forehead to mine, and kisses me. It's soft at first, but when his tears wet my lips, he slides his fingers into my hair to deepen it.

His tongue slips out, seeking entrance, and when I open for him, he releases a strangled groan from deep in his chest. The sound vibrates against my lips and cracks open my chest.

I've put it all out there. I've told him everything. All I can hope for now is that it's not too much to make him walk away again.

He breaks the kiss, his heavy panting warming my skin.

"I'm sorry," he chokes out. "I'm so fuckin' sorry I put you through all of this, and you had to go through it alone."

"Tysin," I whisper. "You couldn't have known this was gonna happen. It's not your fault."

"What if it is, though? What if you were so heartbroken? What if the stress and the anxiety caused you to lose the baby?"

I shake my head. "I blamed myself for a long time. I thought maybe it was my fault, that my body caused this to happen. You can't put this on you. We'll never know why this had to happen."

A weight on my chest lifts at that admission. I've been holding this all in for so long.

"I think what hurt the most was realizing this was the only piece of you I still had, and I lost it too. I thought I was coming around to accepting we would never be together, and it almost felt like I was grieving you twice."

"I'm not going anywhere, Kyla," he croaks, shaking his head feverishly.

He reaches his hand up, looking in my eyes.

"I've spent far too much time running from this and denying how I've felt. I've pushed you away when all I was doing was refusing to accept how I felt and admit what I wanted from the beginning. I love you, Kyla."

With each and every word, the weight on my chest lessens.

"I know I'm not perfect. I've made more mistakes with you than I can count. I can't promise I won't make a few more, but one thing I will promise is never to walk away from you again. I'm done running. I want this, and I want you."

"You do?" My breath feels like it's caught in my throat.

He smiles and nods. "More than anything in this world."

I press my fingers to my mouth, smiling beneath them.

He adjusts his grip, lifting me and moving to stand. I wrap my arms around his neck to hold on. He carries me over to the bed, setting me down on the side, and holds my face in his hands.

"I know it's still early, and there's still so much for us to work through and heal from, but I'm not going anywhere. I haven't given you any reason to trust me, but I'm going to prove to you that it's all behind us."

"Tysin," I whisper against his lips when he leans in to kiss me again. "This right here, it's all I've ever wanted. You. Only you."

He squeezes his eyes shut and exhales a heavy breath. He climbs on the bed with me, pressing his body against my back, and wraps his arm around me to hold me tight.

His palm covers my stomach protectively. There's still so much more for us to talk about, but it was a sign of just how much this meant to him.

It isn't until his breathing evens out and sleep pulls him under that I let myself fully soak in his words.

After lying there for a while, I slip out of bed, knowing there's another man in my life I need to talk to.

Madden's sitting on the patio, flipping his drumsticks while practicing on his drum pad. He spots me opening the door out of the corner of his eye and stops, taking his earbud out.

"Hey. Everything okay?" he asks.

I haven't had a chance to look in the mirror, but I know without looking how puffy my eyes and face are. I've cried more today than I have in a long time. Lord only knows what he must see when he looks at me.

"I'm better than okay."

He relaxes and smiles, and I take the chair next to him. He's dressed in a blue tank top and a pair of black Dickies shorts, barefoot. My brother is one of the most handsome men I know, and the dimple on his cheek is known to affect the ladies.

"It's been a while since we talked about what happened," I say, not mentioning what I'm talking about specifically. We both know already. "It's hard to think back to that time, but I want you to know how much it meant to have you there for me. You've always been there, looking out for me, protecting me. I'm sorry I didn't come to you sooner and tell you about my relationship with Tysin."

His face softens, and he reaches his hand out across the table to squeeze mine. "You know, I was never trying to chase them away. I only wanted the one who deserved you to fight for you. If he was willing to go through me, I figured I could trust he'd stand tall by your side through the hard times too."

I chuckle and shake my head. "Oh, so you weren't just trying to torture me and make sure I ended up single for the rest of my life?"

He shrugs and leans against the back of his chair.

"Like that would ever happen." He smirks. "I've been fighting them off with sticks since we were teenagers."

I narrow my eyes and playfully slap him on the arm.

"Oww," he jokes, rubbing the spot I hit him. I knew better than to think it hurt, even if he did deserve it.

"Does this mean the two of you are official?" he asks.

I nod. "Yeah, we are."

He grins. "I'm happy for you both. Seriously. I get I was upset at first, and at the moment, it was more how it all came out and the fact everyone else seemed to know. I didn't realize it was this serious between the two of you. Tysin deserves to be with someone like you, someone who will love him and care for him. He's never had that before. Tysin's a good friend. He's loyal to the people who are loyal to him. I have no doubt he'll make you happy."

"He does make me happy. It almost feels like a dream. It hasn't always been easy between us, but this is all I've ever wanted."

We both move to stand, and he pulls me in for a hug. His tall stature and his muscular arms nearly swallow me whole.

"It's obvious he makes you happy. Your smile when you talk about him, it's different."

He pats me on the back and steps away.

"I've been in love with him for as long as I can remember."

"Yeah, sis, I know." He chuckles, shaking his head.

If he ever had any inkling about how I felt, he's never let on. Although, I wouldn't be surprised if he picked up on it over the years.

"Like I said before, if he hurts you, I'll have no problem kicking his ass too."

Let's just hope it doesn't get to that point.

CHAPTER TWENTY-EIGHT

KYLA

The last two weeks on the road flew by quickly, and before I knew it, we were pulling our bus back into Carolina Beach. Thankfully, the conversation between Madden and Tysin put any fears and concerns he had about us exploring our relationship to bed.

I was thankful for it because after the roller coaster we've been on to get this far, I didn't want to have to hide how I felt about him anymore.

It's crazy to think how much changed in the three months I was gone. Now I'm back home, trying to make sense of the next steps in life and where to go from here.

Only now, I'm doing it with Tysin by my side.

We may have had a rocky start to our relationship, but we both knew we didn't want to let go of what we had anymore. We decided to take things one step at a time and enjoy just living our life and spending time together, especially before he leaves again.

This is our last weekend before the guys fly out to LA to start recording their next album. I would be lying if I said I wasn't worried about the distance. We both saw what space did to my relationship with Canon.

It all comes back to trusting each other, which is something we're still working on considering how things got started. Plus, our separation wasn't going to be for long. My lease would be up at the end of this month, and then I was moving my things into his place and flying out to be with him.

Tysin opened up to me more about his relationship with his mom and how Madden paid her off to keep her away. When he brought up me coming with him and how he wanted to stay far away from Carolina Beach, it didn't take much convincing from there.

I didn't care where we ended up as long as we were together. Bonus points for the fact Ivy wouldn't be far either since Brix lived in the same city too.

Which brought up the question of where did I go from here now that I wasn't working as their tour manager? It had taken me a while to figure out what I wanted to do now that the tour was behind me. Madden suggested I take on the role of managing the band.

I was hesitant at first, not wanting my job to interfere with my relationship with Tysin. He was quick to put that to rest. In fact, they all did. They were starting to learn quickly it was hard to find people you could trust in the industry.

When Madden told me there was no one better suited for the job who would look out for their best interests, the rest of the guys agreed. I couldn't turn them down.

It wasn't what my dad had in mind when I told him I landed a job, but I wasn't about to start caring now.

Word must've gotten out that we were back in town. Canon reached out a week after, asking if we could meet up to return some things he still had of mine. I had already begun packing his stuff knowing I would have to give it back to him eventually.

As hard as it was to go through, when I pulled away from his house that night, I couldn't ignore the sense of peace that washed over me. I've told myself all along everything would fall into place eventually.

At the time, it felt like my world was crashing down around me, but I knew things would work out in the end.

Tysin: Are you ready for our date tonight, baby?

I bite my lip, staring down at my phone as I gaze out onto the water rolling in along the shoreline. It's a quiet night. The sun is starting to set, turning the sky a mixture of orange, pink, and purple.

This is what I missed about being back home. The sun in my face, the sea-salt air, and the sound of the waves rolling in with the tide. My feet dangle over the edge of the dock outside of Breaking Waves.

While I don't work here anymore, it's still one of my favorite places to come when I need a minute to myself.

Me: What do you have in mind?

My face warms at the thought of him planning something for us.

Tysin: It's a surprise. Now get your sexy ass over here. Bring a change of clothes. I need you here tonight.

I wave to Garrett as I pass by the store, the French doors open to the small patio overlooking the beach. He's standing behind the counter and lifts his hand to wave back.

I dash across the parking lot toward my car and hop in, putting on my sunglasses to shield my eyes from the summer sun.

I swing by my place quickly to freshen up and grab a change of clothes. There were a few nights after the tour ended when we stayed at our own places, but when Tysin told me he missed having me next to him when he slept, I made a promise that for as long as we're in the same town, he'll never go to bed without me beside him.

He must be watching for me because as soon as I pull into his driveway twenty minutes later, he opens the door and jogs down the steps.

"Hi." I grin, stepping out of my car. He reaches for my bag when I use my foot to kick my door shut and pushes me against it, kissing me breathless.

When he pulls back, he tilts his forehead against mine. "Hi."

"I wasn't expecting you to meet me outside." I giggle.

"You were taking too long. I was getting impatient."

My brows shoot up, and I smile. "Impatient for what exactly?"

"C'mon." He laughs. "I'll show you."

I follow him up the steps leading into his house.

I still haven't been able to get over how beautiful the place is. It's very much a bachelor pad, but when I found out he bought a spot overlooking the ocean not far from where we spent our first date, I swear it did funny things to my heart.

My mouth drops open when we walk inside. He steps to the side of the entryway to let me see the path of lit candles leading out onto the patio.

He knows I love sitting outside, watching the waves roll in. There's nothing quite like it.

"Did you do all this for me?"

He nods. "There's no one else on this earth I'd be doing stuff like this for." He laughs.

Tears prick my eyes. He drops my bag near the door, and I toe off my shoes before he pulls me into his arms.

"You like to play it off like you aren't this sweet and romantic man, but this right here proves otherwise."

He winks. "Only for you."

He tilts his head down and presses a kiss against my lips. I reach up, circling my arms around his neck, and hold him to me.

"If you keep doing this, we'll never get to enjoy our date," he jokes.

I sigh and nod, stepping back. He runs his hand down my forearm, laces his fingers in mine, and leads me down the walkway onto the patio.

I inhale a sharp breath, slapping my hand over my mouth when I see the flowers surrounding the table set up in the middle with candles scattered throughout.

Soft music plays in the background.

When he turns around and looks at me, gauging my reaction, I pull him back toward me and kiss him to try to fend off melting into a puddle of tears.

"You didn't have to do all this," I whisper against his mouth. "I love you for it, though. This is so sweet."

He kisses me again, circling his arms around my waist.

When he pulls back, I'm unable to hide the tears threatening to spill over, letting one slip down my cheek. He whispers to me not to cry, rubbing his thumb over the apple of my cheek.

I hadn't noticed it at first, but he must've timed it perfectly, noticing the two stainless-steel lids covering our plates.

He planned everything about the night, down to timing dinner to be ready for when I'd be here.

Tysin leads me over to my chair, pulling it out for me, then bends down to peck a kiss against my lips once more before taking the seat next to mine.

"I can't believe you did all this," I say again when he lifts the lid on our dinners. "Did you cook this too?"

He grins and nods. "I have a lot of talents, some I have yet to reveal to you."

It isn't until after dinner that I realize what he truly means by those words.

He wipes his mouth on a napkin, setting it on the table next to his plate. He circles around the table to where his guitar sits perched on the stand.

Butterflies take flight in my stomach when I watch him lift it into his arms, joining me again at the table.

"I've been working on something for a while now, and I want to play it for you."

He reaches his hand out toward me, pulling me in to kiss him. It isn't until I settle back in my seat that I finally notice the nerves on his face.

I've watched him play hundreds of times, between practicing in our garage growing up to the countless shows I've attended.

When his fingers strum over the guitar, moving without thought, his body finally relaxes. He closes his eyes, and when the words flow from his mouth, my jaw drops open at the sound of his voice.

I remember a long time ago when he told me he could sing and promised to sing for me one day. My heart could've never prepared me for this moment, though.

There's a pained look on his face as if the words physically hurt him. His voice was low and rough, singing about loving someone you'll never have.

I felt the urge to stop him, hating how tortured he looked as if feeling every word flowing from his mouth. Despite how hard it was, I let him finish.

The tempo changes, the pace moves slower, and his voice drops lower.

I may never be deserving of you, of your love, but I'll fight to be.

Tears spill from my eyes. I move the napkin from my lap, tossing it on the table, and wrap my arms around his neck, crashing into him.

His eyes are closed, and he doesn't see me coming.

"When did you write this?" I whisper.

"When we were out on tour," he mumbles.

He moves his guitar to set it down next to him and pulls me into his arms. I straddle his lap, slipping my arms around him, and bury my face into his neck.

"Please don't cry," he whispers. "I wasn't trying to upset you."

"It's hard to hear, to see the look on your face when you're singing it. The words, they were so painfully beautiful. I didn't think I'd ever hear you sing."

"I promised you a long time ago I would."

I press my palms to the side of his face, staring him in the eye. He was showing me he would live up to every promise he's made.

"You keep saying how you don't deserve me, but it's not true." I stare straight into his eyes. "There's no one else in this world I want to be with, no one else I want to love but you."

He stares over my shoulder, lost in thought. I turn him back to face me, pressing a kiss to his mouth.

"I can't promise I won't make mistakes, but I won't stop proving how much I love you."

His fingers grip my hips, holding me against him.

"That's all I want. You. You're all I want."

"Promise?"

"I promise. Forever," I whisper before my lips crash against his.

EPILOGUE

TYSIN
TWO MONTHS LATER

I never thought I'd see the day, but I have to admit it's good to be back home in Carolina Beach.

Even better, it's good to be back with Kyla, playing our very first show at Whiskey Barrel since we got together.

The last few weeks have been some of the best of my life. We've spent our time between LA and traveling to promote our newest music video, taking us back on the road.

It took some cajoling on Kyla's part, but she managed to convince me to share the song I wrote on tour with the guys. What started off as an escape out on the road led me to writing one of my favorite songs.

The guys loved it too, and we agreed to add it to our next album.

I fully expected it to be a song Brix would take the lead on singing, but it made me feel good to hear him agree it was meant for me to sing.

The crowd at Whiskey Barrel tonight is electric. I swear, there's nothing like playing back home at our old stomping grounds.

After we finish our set, I'm desperate for a cold beer to help cool me down. The crowd sticks around, the speakers blaring one of my favorites by Linkin Park.

I swipe a bottle of beer from the bucket left on the table for us and pop the top, taking a heavy swig when Kyla saunters into the back room. I slip my arm around her waist, dragging her into my arms, and she scrunches up her nose when she presses her hand against my sweat-soaked shirt.

"Mmm, hi, baby," I mutter, tucking my head into her neck and taking a deep breath. Her familiar scent is a mix of her floral perfume and the smell of her shampoo, hitting me like a breath of fresh air.

"Hi," she murmurs.

She rocks on her heels, wrapping her hands around my neck, and pulls me close to her.

"You ready to get out of here yet?" I trail kisses along her shoulder and whisper in her ear, "I'm ready to get you home, peel off these clothes, and fuck you until we both pass out."

She trails her finger down the side of my face, her eyes looking deep into mine. She drags her lip between her teeth, fighting off her grin.

I spin her around, caging her back against the wall. She moans against my mouth before I kiss her. My fingers itch to touch her. I slip the bottle of beer into my back pocket and lift her in my arms, pinning her against the wall.

"Tysin," she breathes out, and I dive into her mouth.

Kissing, sucking, and nipping at her lips. She bites mine, and I growl, reaching one hand up to grip her chin between my fingers. Her eyes blaze, and she tilts her head back, granting me access to her neck. I'm tempted to wrap my hand around it and remind her who she belongs to.

"Ahem." A throat clears behind me, and I know without looking it's Trey. He stepped outside for a cigarette after we wrapped up.

"Read the room, man," I mutter, lowering Kyla to her feet. "You couldn't give us a few minutes without going back to being a cockblocker?"

"Listen, just because Madden is over you fuckin' his sister doesn't mean he won't be pissed when he comes back here and sees that shit."

Kyla presses her fingers to her mouth to cover her laughter, her chest still heaving from our kiss.

"Hey now. If he's gonna be mad about anything, it's gonna be your face splattered all over the front page of Hollywood Tea. Don't go blamin' his shitty mood on us," Kyla scoffs.

Slipping my hand behind my back, I grab my beer and lift it in the air to cheer.

"She's gotta point there." I laugh.

Trey grits his teeth, stalking over to the bucket, and swipes a beer. He's been trying to cool it on drinking since the media started dragging his name in the headlines.

There's no doubt this is getting under his skin, pushing him to his breaking point.

"If it's not one thing, it's another," he mutters, popping the top and downing half the bottle.

When we wrapped up our tour, we all headed back home to unwind. While the rest of us came back to CB, Trey decided to spend the week in Nashville with his mom.

At least that's the story he told us.

Turns out the chick he hooked up with back in Philly, Layken, is from Nashville too. I didn't want to pry too much, didn't think it was my business, but I guess he saw some guy feelin' her up. One thing led to another, and Trey dragged the guy's ass out of the bar, and it led to a fistfight.

He insists it didn't go down the way the media claims, but that's the story anyway.

"Listen, it's only a matter of time before your name gets dragged through the mud. It's the way it is. Sounds like the bastard had it comin'. It could've easily been me."

I never would've thought of Trey as someone who'd throw down, but it turns out he is.

Madden's been on edge all day, and Kyla's been fielding phone call after phone call, putting out fires.

Trey wasn't wrong when he said it would set Madden off if he walked in to find me grinding against his sister. I didn't give a fuck anymore, though.

Brix, Ivy, and Madden step through the back door. Brix is holding Ivy's hand, the smile she's been wearing since he proposed permanently plastered on her face.

"We're gonna hit the road. I'm ready to get her ass home." He grins, looking down at Ivy before turning back to us.

Kyla pulls Ivy into a hug and whispers something in her ear. She nods when she leans back, and Ivy smiles at her before looking over at me and winks.

What the hell was that about?

Ivy steps in front of Trey next, wrapping her arm around his waist to hug him. Brix's eyes darken.

"All right, all right. That's enough," Brix barks.

Trey smirks when Ivy pulls back. He crosses his arms over his chest and stares down at the ground. It's obvious he has a lot on his mind.

"You gonna be okay tonight?" Ivy asks.

Trey nods. "Yeah, sis, I'll be good."

We've all gotten closer since being out on the road together. It's hard not to when you're all crammed on the same bus.

"I wouldn't let this shit bother you," Madden adds. "Hollywood Tea makes their money off every click they get. They don't give a shit whether the garbage they are spewing is true if it means bringing in more money."

Trey shakes his head and sighs. "I'm just sorry you guys are gettin' dragged into it."

I step in front of Trey and reach my hand out to shake his. He claps me on the back.

"Don't worry about it, man. We've all been there. Don't let it get under your skin."

"You know what they say," Brix adds. "There's no such thing as bad press."

Ivy rolls her eyes. "Says the attention-seeking rebel."

Brix curls his lip, reaches his hand out for hers, and yanks Ivy into his arms. She throws her head back and laughs when he lifts her and carries her out, Ivy waving goodbye behind him.

"Let's go grab another beer." Madden gestures toward the bar, and Trey nods.

"We're gonna head out." My eyes flicker over to Kyla's, and she presses her lips together.

Madden notices and shakes his head. "Get the fuck outta here," he bellows.

Abel is standing outside the door waiting for us as Brix and Ivy pull out of the parking lot. He leads us over to my car. We parked out back, avoiding the crowd and fans trying to sneak past to get to us.

"I'm gonna drive." Kyla reaches for my key, snatching it from my hand. "You've been drinking."

"I don't think so, baby." I wrap my arms around her waist, reaching for the keys behind her back. "I've only had one drink. I'm good to drive."

"It's not worth risking it. It's not that far." Her voice drops. "Plus, don't you want to see me behind the wheel of your car?"

I narrow my eyes, and she reaches her other hand out, running her palm over the front of my jeans.

I thrust my hip against her. "Trust me, Kyla. I'd love nothing more than to watch you behind the wheel, but not this car."

"You don't trust me?" She huffs, trying to wear me down.

She moves her hand, gripping my dick through my jeans. I flare my nostrils and growl.

She glances over my shoulder to where Abel stands. I check behind me to find him with his arms crossed near the door, watching over us.

My back is to him, hiding the way she strokes my dick, and I'm ready to bend her over the hood of my Venom GT and spank her ass right here.

She yawns, releasing her hold to stretch her arms over her head. "Yeah, okay. I guess I'm feeling tired. We can head home and call it a night."

I grip her hip, pulling her close to my body. She leans her head back, giving me full access to her neck, and I trail my nose over her sensitive skin.

"It's too bad you said no, though." She swallows hard. "It kind of spoils what else I had in mind."

"Get the fuck in the car, Kyla."

She giggles, pulling back. She tempts me, stepping around to the driver's side door. She lifts the key in her hand and waves them.

"Last chance, my way or the highway." She snickers.

I shake my head, taking a deep breath, and stalk around to the passenger side.

"Get in," I grit. "Now."

She grins, hitting the keypad to unlock the door, and climbs inside.

Her eyes are wide, her face beaming when she shuts the door behind her. There's a light on in the parking lot a few feet away, casting enough of a glow into the car for me to get a good look at her face.

She rubs her hands together before she shoves the key in the ignition, and the car roars to life.

I lean over and press my mouth to her ear. "Be careful."

She revs the engine, and I brush my hand over the front of her jeans.

Her body tenses and her legs fall open.

"Mmm, is that what you want?" I grin. "You want me to make you come right here?"

"Tysin," she mutters breathlessly.

"Or should I make you drive us home, and I can torture you there for not listening?"

Her mouth curls up. "Both."

I pop the button of her jeans and unzip them. Her body trembles, staring down at my hand before I reach into her panties.

She rolls her eyes shut and tilts her head back.

"God, yesss," she hisses.

"That feel good, baby?" I moan against her ear. "My girl is wet for me. Is that why you're tryin' to get under my skin?"

"Sin," she groans, and I close my eyes, letting the sound of her throaty voice wash over me.

My voice drops. "Push your pants down, Kyla."

She looks around the car, checking to see if anyone is around before she obliges. She unzips them the rest of the way and shoves them over her hips to her knees. Her legs fall open, and she leans back against the seat.

I brush my finger over her clit, and her mouth drops open, but no sound comes out.

“So wet,” I growl. “All mine.”

“All yours.”

I dip my finger into her tight pussy, brushing my thumb over her clit, and her arm shoots out to grip my forearm.

When I twist my wrist and curl my finger, hitting that delicious spot inside her, she starts to tremble.

“You want to come, Kyla?” I growl in her ear.

She nods, frantic, her breaths coming out in deep, heavy pants.

“Say it. I want to hear you say the words.”

“Yesss. Please, Tysin. Make me come,” she begs. “Please.”

I rub her clit slowly in circles, flicking my finger once more, and her body shudders with the force of her release.

She digs her nails into my arm, breaking the surface. I moan at the sweet pain, loving her marks on my skin.

“My sweet pussy,” I snarl, lifting my soaked fingers to my mouth.

“Yours, Tysin. Always yours.”

Always mine.

Do you want more of Tysin and Kyla?

Sign up to receive their bonus epilogue at:

www.authorbrookeobrien.com/tysin

Don't forget to grab **SINS OF A REBEL**, an optional prequel novella, if you want to go back to where it all began.

Thank you for reading **TYSIN**! I hope you love Tysin and Kyla as much as I do. If you enjoyed their story, I would appreciate your help in spreading the word, including telling a friend. Reviews help readers find books! Please leave a review on your favorite site.

You can continue the A Rebels Havoc series with **TREY**, Trey and Layken's story. It's a surprise pregnancy, rock star romance.

Grab the rest of the series at www.authorbrookeobrien.com/arebelshavoc today!

Now, turn the page for a sneak peek of Torn...

Torn

A TATTERED HEART DUET #1

USA TODAY BESTSELLING AUTHOR

BROOKE O'BRIEN

Prologue

MAVERICK

It was never my intention to fall in love with my best friend's sister. I was thirteen when I moved down the street from Dean Blake. He had come into my life at a time I struggled to cope with the world around me. Our friendship came without any pressures, it was easy. He didn't ask questions, but I think he knew what would happen if he did.

I closed off the door to my heart a long time ago. I didn't want to feel. The pain that comes with letting the emotions in is more than I could ever bear. Even through it all, I still remember the way I felt when I met his twin sister, Ryan. It was like a jolt to my heart, forcing it to beat out of rhythm.

Ryan was all legs, chocolate brown hair flowing in the breeze covered by her backward snapback. The first thing I noticed was the intricate detail of the designs covering her skin, like vines wrapping around her arm.

If the sweet and innocent look on her face was any indication, she was too young to have tattoos of her own. I was drawn to the outward shell she presented to the world because I recognized it for what it was. A distraction from all the parts you want to keep buried deep. She was like a mirage of walking contradictions, which I knew to be true the moment she opened her smart mouth.

The passion she withheld under the surface was like a beacon of light shining in the dark night. Her fiery personality was the first thing to trigger a spark in the hollows of my heart.

All these years I've spent keeping my distance from her, out of fear of facing my feelings and the consequences that could follow. The hard part is, I know she feels the connection between us, too. The pull that keeps us tethered to each other, despite never allowing her to get close enough.

She's turning eighteen in two days and the resistance I've been struggling to keep hold of is starting to wear thin. Nothing good can come from going down this path because no matter how much my heart aches for her, it's inevitable I'll leave her heart torn in two.

Chapter One

RYAN

"Roll the window down, it smells like sex in here!" I shout, waving my hand in front of my face. Sticking my head outside, I take a deep breath and turn my head toward my best friend with a shit eating grin on my face.

"Says the virgin," she mutters, rolling her eyes as she turns up the music to drown out any smart-ass reply I could fire back. I know she can hear me as I tell her to fuck off, which prompts her to wave her middle finger in the air at me while keeping her eyes on the road.

Papa Roach blares through the speakers, as I slide back into my seat adjusting my hat as I do. I can feel the energy from the music run through my body as I nod my head to the lyrics.

Nadia is my best friend, my A1 since day one. There's not much I wouldn't do for her and I knew it to be true from the day we first met.

We were in eighth grade, riding the bus to school, when Kara Parker thought it would be fucking funny to pick shit out of the garbage and throw it at me from where she sat in the back. She only messed with me on the days my twin brother, Dean, would opt to walk to school with his friends.

She knew better than to pull that shit around Dean.

Nadia had been sitting in the seat across from me. It was the first day we had ever talked to each other. After watching a pop bottle cap whiz past our heads, she turned toward me with her face hard as stone as she said, "You ready to put this bitch down?"

My response mirrored the same devilish grin she flashed me. She's been my ride or die ever since.

"Did you talk to your mom about staying over at my place tomorrow?" she asks, shouting over the music. Nadia's parents take on the role of parenting from a distance. They leave her money on the counter and make sure there's always food in the cabinets. Otherwise, they're hardly home, which makes it the perfect place to crash when we plan to hit up a party or two on the weekends.

"She hasn't responded to my text message yet," I mutter, clicking the button on the side of my phone to check for a response. "I'm going to call her and see." Leaning over, I turn down the radio as I click the call button.

"Big Papa's Pizzeria."

My brother's immature greeting has me rolling my eyes so hard I'm surprised they didn't pop out of my head and roll across the floor. The worst part is the annoying laugh that follows finding his lame joke funny.

"Put Mom on the phone," I snap, cutting off his obnoxious laughter, running my fingers over the frayed hole in my jeans.

"What's in it for me?"

"Staying alive. Now quit being a prick, dick licker, and put her on the phone."

"You wanna talk to your mom with that dirty mouth?" Dean laughs. I can hear the light chuckling in the background, and if I had to guess, Maverick is there with him.

Figures.

"Seriously, D. I don't have all night. If I don't talk to her now, I'm going to be home late."

"You better hope that's not the case. After the last time, you know you're going to end up grounded. Happy Birthday to you."

I can picture his smug face as he sings the last part to me and I seriously want to junk punch him.

"Alright, Dad. Noted. Now put her on the fucking phone."

I can hear the light rustling on the other end before my mom's overly chipper voice filters through the phone.

"Yes, Ryan," she says with a sigh.

"Hi, Mom," I reply, my tone extra sweet which has Nadia laughing. "Is it cool if I crash at Nadia's this weekend?"

"Not tonight, Ryan," she replies curtly. "You can tomorrow since it's your birthday, but it's not necessary to stay over two nights in a row."

"Can I stay out a little later tonight then instead? It's a Friday night and we were going to meet up with some friends."

"You've been late once already this month, even after I extended your curfew. You have until ten o'clock to be home, Ryan. By the looks of it, that gives you seventeen minutes. I'll see you soon."

Nadia glances down at the clock as the line disconnects.

"Ry, we're not going to make it in time," she says, voicing my thoughts. I don't say anything because she's right. My house is at least twenty-five minutes away on a good day.

"Shit," I groan, running my hand over my face.

Nadia does her best to get me home in time, but when we hit a train on Rockford Drive, I know it's no use.

"Look on the bright side," Nadia says, peering over at me out of the corner of her eye. "If Dean is home, that likely means Maverick is crashing at your house tonight."

Maverick is one of my brother's best friends, which is both a blessing and a curse. He and Dean never go anywhere without the other. Dean is the annoying, obnoxious jock who likes to have all the attention on him. Maverick, on the other hand, is the complete opposite and sometimes I wonder what prompted their friendship.

Don't get me wrong, Dean's my twin brother, and he's a great guy. I don't know what they have in common besides skateboarding. Whatever it is, they are nearly inseparable. Maverick usually ends up staying over at our house, which I appreciate because it means I get to see him more.

"Like that matters. He acts as if I'm not there. I swear you'd think he hated me or something."

"I don't think that's true." Nadia laughs, shaking her head. "I think he's very much aware you're there. He just knows Dean would lose his shit if he knew he saw you as anything but his sister."

Which brings me to why it's a curse. Any chance of Maverick seeing me as more than his best friend's sister goes out the window. I know he would never do anything to put their friendship in jeopardy.

I can keep a secret and what Dean doesn't know won't hurt him.

Nadia whips the car into the driveway, pulling in behind Dean's beat-up Ford truck. The thing has seen better days, but he refuses to replace it.

"Text me when you can and let me know the damage," she mutters, clearly concerned our plans for tomorrow could be ruined.

I push the door of the car open and lean the seat forward, pulling out my skateboard from the backseat. I sling my backpack over my shoulder and readjust my hat on my head.

"Wish me luck," I groan, as I move the seat back in place.

We say our goodbyes as I head toward the front of my house.

My mom is in the kitchen loading the dishwasher when I enter the house. She doesn't bother to look at me, which I know can't be good. Kicking my shoes off near the door, I prop my board against the wall.

I spot Dean and Maverick lounging in the living room. Dean has his leg draped across the coffee table and a grin on his face, knowing what's about to come. Maverick grimaces and I know this can't be good.

"Welcome home," my mother says, the force of the dishwasher closing draws my attention away from him.

"Ryan, this is the second time you've been late this month. Before you even try to argue, I want to point out your birthday is in less than two hours, and I know you have plans with Nadia."

Dropping my bag down on the bench near the door, I slide the hat off my head and toss it on top before facing my mom.

"I'm sorry," I sigh, knowing nothing good will come from me saying anything more. "I'm going to bed."

I walk through the kitchen and into the living room. The urge to junk punch Dean has returned when I see the arrogant smirk on his face.

"Keep it up, fucker," I mutter under my breath, careful to not let my mom overhear us as I flash him the finger.

"What's that?" he retorts, turning his head to peer over the back of the couch.

Spinning around, I find both of their eyes on me. Seeing that my mom has since made her way out of the kitchen, likely retreating to our parents' bedroom, I don't hold back.

"I said keep it up, fucker. I should be the one laughin' at you, sitting at home like a bum on a Friday night," I snap, sounding bored as I lean against the wall.

There are about seven minutes separating the two of us. My parents were expecting to bring home two baby boys when I was born. What they didn't expect was for the second child to be born a girl. My name is evidence of that.

Dean turns around, facing the TV and lets out an annoyed grunt, "Fuck off, Ry."

My eyes bounce from Dean to Maverick and I'm surprised when I find Maverick's are already on me. They shine bright with amusement, as he bites his lower lip in an attempt to hide the grin lining his mouth. Crossing his arms over his chest, he runs his hand over his jaw as he glances over to make sure Dean isn't paying attention.

The thick muscles are tanned from all his days outside without his T-shirt on. His dark-brown hair is longer on top. The wayward strands give the appearance like he has ran his fingers through them one too many times.

The sleeves of my white T-shirt are cut off, giving it more of a muscle-shirt look. You can see my black sports bra from the side and a hint of my sun-kissed skin underneath.

My heart starts to pound as I relish the thought of him struggling to take his eyes off me. Taking two steps backward, I keep my eyes trained on him. I think back to my conversation with Nadia in the car when she said it's Dean that's holding him back.

The bold side of me wants to test her theory and see if it's true.

Standing outside my bedroom door, I keep my eyes focused on Maverick as I grab the hem of my shirt and pull the cotton material over my head. I roll my shirt into a ball before tossing it in the direction of my dirty clothes but not bothering to check if it made it.

I watch as Maverick's jaw clenches as his eyes travel over the length of my body, resting longer on my chest than necessary before finally bringing his eyes up to meet mine. He leans forward, pressing his elbows to his knees. Even then, he doesn't take his eyes off me.

"D, I'm gonna use your bathroom quick and head out. I should've been home a little while ago."

I can hear Dean mumble out a response, but I have no idea what he says. I'm too lost in the look on Maverick's face to pay much attention to what is going on around me.

Bracing his palms on his knees, Maverick moves to stand. He's so tall, standing over six feet. He's athletic, but whereas my brother is stockier from his time in football, Maverick is lean.

I can hear my heart pounding in my ears as he stalks toward me with a slight tic in his jaw. The closer he gets to me, the more my body comes alive with his presence.

"A little bold of you. Wouldn't you say, Rebel?"

It isn't the first time I've heard him use the nickname, but the tone in his voice is deeper. I can feel the words roll through me, crashing over me like waves as he stands close leaving only an inch between us.

I'm not able to think properly as I stare up at his gray eyes. They're so dark, it's almost like a storm is brewing in their depths.

Raising his hand up, he runs his knuckle along the soft skin of my shoulder as I force a step away from him. I need to gain some semblance of sanity, but the move causes his lip to curl in a small grin.

"You have nothing to say now? I didn't think that was possible." His quiet chuckle does crazy things to my heart.

"Aren't you supposed to be leaving now?" I retort, hating how he can look so unaffected knowing the way he's making me feel.

"Yeah, I am. Are you sure it's what you want though?"

He presses the palm of his hand against my hip as he moves to step closer in the narrow hallway. I'm standing so close to the wall, I know there's plenty of room for him to pass by.

His thumb lightly traces my exposed skin, as he takes a step around me. His body is pressed against mine, bringing us closer than we've ever been.

The move forces the air out of my chest and I know he can feel my body tremble beneath his touch.

"I didn't think so," he whispers against the shell of my ear.

As soon as he passes by me and the bathroom, he glances back at me. His eyes travel down to where my chest heaves with every struggled breath before looking back up at me. Flashing me a wink, he turns and walks down the hallway and out the front door without another word.

Holy shit.

Do you want more Maverick and Ryan?

Check out the today!

BOOKS BY BROOKE

A Rebels Havoc Series

Brix
Sins of a Rebel (Prequel to Tysin)
Tysin
Trey
Madden

Men of Blaze

Personal Foul
Reckless Rebound (Cocky Hero Club)

Tattered Heart Duet

Torn
Tattered

A Heart's Compass Series

Where I Found You
Lost Before You
Until I Found You
Now That I Found You
Sacrifice (Salvation Society)

Standalones (In order of publication)

Wild Irish

Learn more and purchase your copy at:

www.authorbrookeobrien.com/booksbybrooke

ACKNOWLEDGMENTS

My Boys – I love you more than anything on this earth. Everything I do is for you.

To my AMAZING beta readers – Kristen, Donna, Summer, April, and Ana. Thank you for reading Tysin and Kyla's story before anyone else, for your honest feedback, and helping me make their story better. I'm so grateful for you! <3

Jenny Sims and Rox LeBlanc – I've enjoyed working with and learning from you! Thank you for all your hard work on this project and helping me learn along the way.

To the fantastic bloggers and my Rebel Release Team, thank you for being a part of this one. I'm excited to hear what you think of Tysin and Kyla. I hope you know how grateful I am for every one of you.

My Rebels Readers – I love being able to connect with all of you in my Reader Group and across social media. Thank you for your love of this series. It's truly changed my life and I'm so thankful for you all!

April – Thank you so much for your friendship. We've grown close over the past couple years and I'm so thankful to have you in my life, both as a book friend and a real friend.

Kristen – You keep it real with me, always! I can't begin to put into words how much I appreciate you being there for me. You helped me get this story to where it is today and keeping me focused and motivated in times where I'd never finish. Thanks for riding my ass when I need it, but also reminding me to be patient with myself too.

Kate Jessop and Lyssa Cole – Thank you for your friendship and support, for checking in with me and letting me bounce ideas off you. Your friendship and support mean the world to me.

ABOUT BROOKE

Brooke O'Brien is an author of steamy and swoon-worthy contemporary romances.

She believes a love worth having is worth fighting for, and she brings this into her stories where her characters risk it all for love.

If Brooke's not writing or reading, she's probably spending time with her family, binge-watching the latest crime documentary, indulging in chocolate, or watching Hawkeye football or NBA basketball.

She loves to interact with readers! Keep in touch with Brooke by following her on social media, subscribe to her newsletter, and join her exclusive Reader Group at: .

COPYRIGHT

TYSIN

Visit my website at www.authorbrookeobrien.com.

Edited by Jenny Sims, Editing4Indies
Proofread by Rox LeBlanc with Rox's Reads

Cover Design by Dee Garcia, Black Widow Designs
Version: BMO09152022